ON THE RUN

The interval between guard stations took them across a wide boulevard that offered a direct view of the Imperial Palace. It looked like a magnificent wedding cake that had been mistreated by small boys. Pieces of icing had crumbled to lower levels, and here and there someone had pushed in a finger for a taste of frosting.

At the next guard station, a police dog stopped them. Karff presented his credentials to the fiber-optic eye extending from the dog's collar.

"Excuse me, Colonel Karff," said the computer in the command collar, "but we have a little problem here. Could you step inside the station house, please?" Karff looked at Detana and then back at the dog.

"Of course," he said, "but I am pressed for time."

"This should not take long..."

Also by Alexis A. Gilliland
Published by Ballantine Books:

LONG SHOT FOR ROSINANTE

THE PIRATES OF ROSINANTE

THE REVOLUTION FROM ROSINANTE

The End Of The Empire

Alexis A. Gilliland

A Del Rey Book

BALLANTINE BOOKS • **NEW YORK**

*This book is dedicated
to those heroic bureaucrats,
Sir Domenic Flandry of Imperial Terra
and Jame Retief of the CDT.*

A Del Rey Book

Published by Ballantine Books

Library of Congress Catalog Card Number: 83-90782

ISBN 0-345-31334-8

Printed in Canada

First Edition: December 1983

Cover art by Ralph McQuarrie

Contents

Prologue

THE FIRST EMPEROR of the Holy Human Empire, Franz-Otto I, called The Great, had, in his youth, been trained as a forester. He understood that in a forest it is impossible to define a clear boundary line. And in his Empire, which was neither Holy, nor wholly Human, nor an Empire, the fuzzy borders and the diffuse and tenuous lines of communication and authority did not bother him. Indeed, he often remarked that it seemed very like a forest. Franz-Otto The Great settled planets where they were fertile, terraformed them where they were not, and took appropriate notice of those that gave him trouble.

Long after his death the Holy Human Empire remained a dispersed and filamentous tangle, a topopolitical mess, the opposite of wieldy, held together by the iron grip of the mature and rigid military technology that had put it together in the first place.

And one fine morning an invention appeared which made revolution possible. Generations of incompetence, venality, and corruption had prepared the ground; the winds of change swept revolution across the depths of space. The Empire was burning.

Chapter 1.
Flight from Portales

SENIOR COLONEL SALOMAN Thibalt Karff arrived at his office early and checked out the overnight accumulation in his in-box, a stack of documents an inch thick. It was colorful, that stack—yellow flags for urgent, red flags for emergency, a blue-and-white-striped flag indicating a matter of Imperial interest. The item he was looking for wasn't there. Forty-eight hours after making a formal request there was nothing! He had half expected to be relieved of his command.

He dropped the stack back in the in-box and hung up his overcoat and hat. The coat had a pile lining, rather than the armor suggested by regulations. He wore a gevlar vest under his shirt and figured that was sufficient. Any extra safety provided by an armored overcoat was more than offset by the extra weight and lack of warmth. Besides, the coat was designed for a pile lining.

He drew himself a cup of coffee and opened the security cabinet to take out his humidor. One cigar left; he cut off the end and sat back in his chair as he lit it.

Well, now, he mused, is it perhaps the time to act? Probably yes. If it wasn't, I would have heard about it. "For retreatism, defeatism, and so forth, you are herewith relieved of your command." Why hadn't the general come down on him? He exhaled cigar smoke in a long sigh. Wrong question. Bloyer *hadn't* come down on him. Don't start asking about his motives. *If* we destroy the files, am I clean? Yes. I said I was going to, and the son of a bitch didn't get back to me in a timely fashion. If it turns out to be a dumb move, is *he* covered? Ehh...he's just moved his office into one of those command transporters for security reasons—he can always say it fell in a crack. Karff took a sip of black coffee. And that's the worst case. The best case is that I'm right about losing the war. In which case,

2

trashing the files will protect the lives of the people I'm responsible for. Hope for the best, expect the worst. He took another sip of coffee. There was still the matter of timing. He could be right, but if he acted prematurely he might be shot. Hell, he decided, I could be shot *anyway*. Pray for forgiveness, not permission. On the whole, it was definitely time to act. Still... mature deliberation was called for. He finished his coffee and his cigar before calling the morning staff meeting.

Karff's officers filed in, taking their seats in the leather armchairs and matching sofa and assorted straight chairs in strict order of rank. Captain Detana, Karff's aide, took his place in the doorway.

"Good morning, gentlemen," Karff said pleasantly. "As some of you may suspect, things have not been going as well as we could wish, lately." There was a slight stir. One did not admit the war was going badly. "Two days ago—" he glanced at his watch, "forty-nine hours, to be precise, I asked headquarters for permission to destroy the files. Formally. Stating in writing that in my best professional judgment it was now time for such an action." He coughed and looked around the room, which was completely silent. "I have had no response. Nothing. Lacking official instructions, I must act as I think best. Gentlemen, it is time to destroy the files!"

"At last an order that makes sense!" Lieutenant Grischa said. Karff ignored him.

"I, myself, will handle the Section C file. Are there any questions?"

"Did General Bloyer approve?" Colonel Prittwitz asked from the depth of the big easy chair.

"My discussion with the general led me to put it in writing. I must tell you that he wasn't too pleased. Nevertheless, he has not disapproved when it is his responsibility to do so in a timely fashion. If, I mean, he does, in fact, disapprove. Is that sufficient, Colonel?" Prittwitz looked dour, but said nothing.

"Colonel Karff, is it true that the Imperial Household has moved off Portales?" Lieutenant Grischa asked.

"Yes, it is." The blue-and-white-striped flag marked the revised schedule of evacuation points for key personnel.

"Where will they go, sir?" Portales was the last Imperial stronghold in a salient extended deep into a region of unfruited stars. All plausible destinations were in Rebel hands.

3

"I expect that information is classified, Lieutenant. And properly so. No more questions? Excellent. Section C backup material has priority at the paper shredder."

"And another interstellar empire goes down the tubes." Detana spoke softly, but Karff scowled at him, and in the sudden silence the crackle of small-arms fire could be heard.

"Rank defeatism is something which I will not tolerate!" Karff said. There was a ripple of nervous laughter. "Meeting dismissed."

As his staff left, he motioned Detana to him. "You could be right, Captain. Post a couple of men on sentry duty. Yellow alert."

Karff activated his desk console and undertook the systematic erasure of the records of the spies, informers, and double agents that had supported his operation. Finishing late in the morning, he began checking and spot checking the work in other sections. He had just keyed into the semisensitive area of procurement auditing when there was an explosion in the hall outside. Karff hit the intercom button for his aide.

"What happened, Detana?"

"Guerillas. Maybe platoon strength."

"The explosion?"

"They overrode the lock on the elevators and came up. We hit them with a grenade when the door opened. You might want to lock your door, sir."

"Casualties?"

"The Civil Guards downstairs. So far. Orders?" Gunfire was reverberating in the hallway outside.

"Shee-it! There's an off-planet evacuation from Checkpoint Tango this evening. Are you interested?"

"At nineteen-thirty hours? Rank defeatism, sir. Lock your damn door."

"Carry on, Detana." Karff cued off the cordless phone and locked his door. Now what? he asked himself. The shooting sounded closer, punctuated by the *whump*! of concussion grenades. He drew his ceremonial officer's pistol. Light, compact, and accurate, but without much stopping power; it suddenly seemed pathetically inadequate, like a child's toy. God, was there any way out of this place? He opened his credenza and took out an emergency fire escape. It was a reel of monofilament operated by a pistol grip attached to a web-belt harness.

He was fastening the end of the filament to the leg of his desk when a civilian wearing a red armband kicked open the door and sprayed the room with machinegun fire. Karff's kneeling position saved him. He raised his pistol and squeezed off one round, hitting the guerilla under the left eye. The bullet exited from the back of the head, spattering blood and brain tissue on the door frame.

Next comes a grenade, thought Karff, belting on the escape harness. He was cranking open the armored window when the phone rang.

The force of habit is very strong. Holstering his automatic, he took the phone with him as he went out the window, unreeling the monofilament from the pistol grip as he rappeled down the sheer face of the building. Outside it was cold but quiet. The shooting above him sounded like a distant television show, unreal and far away.

"Military Counter-Intelligence," he said when the phone continued to ring, "Colonel Karff speaking." There was a pause.

"Karff?" General Bloyer asked at last. He sounded surprised. Who did he expect, thought Karff. Who *did* he expect? "Ah . . . yes," Bloyer continued. "I believe you may have been right the other day, Colonel. It *is* time to destroy the files. I apologize for my remarks about defeatism, but I have, as you know, been under severe pressure, and treason, as they say, is a matter of dates . . ." He babbled on as Karff continued down the wall, shivering in the frigid air. He's stalling, thought Karff. No! The son of a bitch is trying to hear if there's a commando raid going on. He can't ask, and he badly needs to know. He's sold us out to save his ass, but if he can't deliver, he's up shit creek. By the time Karff reached the sidewalk, which was liberally covered with broken glass, Bloyer was explaining in minute and insulting detail how the files ought to be destroyed. Karff hit the release button on the escape harness and watched it rewind itself rather faster than he had come down. Damn, he thought, I don't even have my hat.

"Excuse me, General," he said at last, "we're terribly busy here, and if you *really* want those files destroyed, we ought to get on with it."

"Oh. Oh, yes. Yes, of course. Carry on, Colonel."

Karff cued off the phone and shivered. My hat *and* my

overcoat, he thought. He hit the intercom for Detana. After several rings his aide answered.

"Whattya want, Karff?" Gunfire was clearly audible over the phone.

"Locking my door didn't do it. Can you get to my office?"

"What for?"

"The emergency fire escape. I used it in a hurry and left my hat and coat. Would you pitch them down to me?"

"Emergency fire escape, eh? I'll see what I can do for you, sir."

"What's going on?"

"Colonel Prittwitz is making a stand by the east stairwell, sir. Grischa and I are the strategic reserve."

"Right. Now move it. I'm freezing my ass off down here!"

"Come on, Grischa," Detana shouted, "we've got a better 'ole to go to!"

Karff crouched down beside a large concrete planter, where he could observe without being unduly conspicuous. After a moment his hat and coat sailed out the window, closely followed by Captain Detana, a machine gun in one hand, the pistol grip in the other, and the escape harness in his teeth. A white phosphorous grenade exploded in the room, and dense white smoke poured out of the window as Karff ran over to recover his coat and hat. Above, Detana bounded down the wall. Below, Karff put on his overcoat and replaced his toothbrush in his hat. He was slipping his holstered pistol through the slit in his overcoat when Detana hit the ground.

"What happened?" Karff asked.

"Prittwitz got blown away." His aide slung the captured machine gun across his chest. He pulled the garrison cap from under the shoulder strap of his field jacket and set it at a rakish angle. "Shall I arrange transportation to Checkpoint Tango?"

"We'll improvise, Detana. Let's go."

Detana looked around. There were no signs of life on the street, no vehicles, no people. "Where *is* everybody, sir?"

"The reaction force?" It was conspicuous by its absence. Karff cued the phone and tried calling one of the emergency numbers, but heard only a busy signal. Then the phone went dead. He looked at the useless instrument for a second and threw it away. "I expect the guerillas ambushed them. Or maybe Bloyer put them on detail somewhere. Let's get out of here."

As they walked down into the brightly lit vacway station, they were confronted with a red POWER OFF sign flashing over the turnstile. Detana stopped a civilian, a middle-aged woman with a roll of bedding slung over her shoulder, and asked her what had happened.

"They *have* power," she said. "They've lost vacuum. The tubes aren't tight anymore so the trains can't move. They went down about noon."

"Should I check it with the stationmaster, Colonel?"

"No. I believe her. There's been a lot of sabotage directed at the tubes."

"Yes, sir. Do we wait for them to fix it?"

Karff grimaced. "It takes five, maybe ten minutes to slap an airbag on a hole." He looked at the dispirited people standing around and shook his head. "There must be some other problem. Can we catch a bus?"

"Sure, Colonel. Get me the fuel and I'll give you all the buses you want. Taxis too." The army had requisitioned all available fuel stocks.

"So we walk," Karff concluded. "One of the north–south arborcades ought to be safe enough." The arborcades were lines of block-long greenhouses enclosing row houses and small apartment buildings in a kind of communal atrium. At each end they were secured by a computer-operated guard station, and in the winter they were relatively warm.

They turned into the Princess Bespis Promenade at the west exit from the vacway station and headed south under the fragrant fig-fruit vines that formed a lofty arbor over the wide and spacious parking lot filled with unfueled vehicles. Except for small groups of youths that vanished as they approached, the sidewalks were deserted. The police dogs at the guard station watched them alertly, and once or twice they were challenged. The only sign of violence was a ruined maintenance robot lying on the sidewalk. It had been aloft harvesting fig-fruit when someone shot it down. It lay on the pavement, a broken mechanical thing, the aromatic, purple fig-fruit spilling out of its sheet-metal hopper.

Once the interval between guard stations took them across a wide boulevard that gave them a direct view of the Imperial Palace. It looked like a magnificent wedding cake that had been mistreated by small boys. Pieces of icing had crumbled to lower levels, and here and there someone had pushed in a finger for a taste of frosting.

At the next guard station, a police dog stopped them. Karff presented his credentials to the fiber-optic eye extending from the dog's collar.

"Excuse me, Colonel Karff," said the computer in the command collar it rode over the dog's throat, "but we have a little problem here. Could you step inside the station house, please?"

Karff looked at Detana and then back at the dog.

"Of course," he said, "but I am pressed for time."

"This should not take long," the command collar said. Inside the security station was an automatic feeding machine that dispensed dry dog food on demand. Someone had put a padlock on it.

"The padlock was reported last night," the computer said, "but no one has come to remove it." Several other dogs wearing command collars had gathered around the guard station.

Karff looked at Detana. "Shoot it off?"

"No need, Colonel." From his pocket Detana took a small wallet containing variegated picklocks, selected one, and opened the padlock in a few deft motions. The dog pressed the bar without prompting, and the vending machine pushed out a little tray of dried food, which the dog at once began to wolf down.

"Thank you, Colonel," the command collar said. "May we return the favor?"

"Perhaps." Karff watched the dogs eat for a moment. "We're looking for transportation down to..." He thought a moment and gave the address of Checkpoint Tango.

The command collar accessed the local intelligence files. After a moment it furnished Karff with the name and address of a man who had a truck and fuel to drive it, one of the semi-licit businesses the police winked at when they could.

The late afternoon sky promised snow. In the west, on the Imperial side of the river, an ammunition dump sent a cloud of black smoke billowing upward.

"That's the sewage treatment plant," the truck driver said, "across what's left of the bridge." The bridge had been hit from the air. The supporting structure was badly damaged, twisted ruined metal leaning against cracked and shattered concrete.

The pavement on the bridge was warped and broken, but passable for pedestrians if not vehicles.

"Thanks for the lift." Karff handed him a large bill. "We'll walk from here."

"Why did you tip him, Colonel?" Detana asked as they made their way across the bridge. "He took us at gunpoint."

"The Reichskredit Imperiales isn't worth the paper it's printed on. Why be stingy spending it?"

They walked on in silence. On the other side of the overpass, a burnt-out truck had hit a fire hydrant and sat with its front end frozen in a mound of ice. This is the way the world ends, Karff thought bleakly. Fire or ice. Fire *and* ice. Lose with style. He felt bone tired and chilled to the marrow. Not the honest cold of winter, but the black frost of depression. How long have I been here, he wondered. Long enough for Portales to be home? He shoved his hands in his pockets. If I had a choice, I wouldn't leave it, but if I could go back, would I come *here*? Probably not, he decided, and shivered.

"Son of a bitch," Detana said, "it's *cold!*"

Checkpoint Tango was on the loading platform built over the main hyperbaric reactor, half a hectare of tarmac with low walls on the north and east. Several hundred men and women were gathered in the lee of the dock, huddling around scrapwood bonfires. Judges, lawyers, prosecuting attorneys, middle-class war criminals, Imperial refuse awaiting disposal. They look almost as cheerful as I feel, Karff thought, pushing in toward one of the bonfires.

As he got close enough to feel the warmth, he recognized one of his agents.

"Good evening, ma'am."

"Fancy meeting you here, Colonel." She shifted her grip on her shoulder bag. "Do you think it will snow?"

Karff looked around. "It's already snowing," he said, holding his hands out to the fire. "Hey, you don't have to hang out with *this* lot, you know. Your file is erased."

"The radio said the Rebels took the building, files and all," she said. "Are you sure?"

"I erased the Section C files myself. Just before the raid. Everything. The whole cheese."

"That's good to know, Colonel. I'll take my chances on Portales, then." She opened her shoulder bag and gave him a carefully wrapped sandwich. "Egg salad on a kaiser roll, a most inadequate token of my gratitude."

"Bless you, darling," he said softly. "This has been my day for missing meals."

When Karff looked up from unwrapping the roll she was gone. Beside him stood Detana with his machine gun. Karff handed him half the sandwich.

"It's late," Detana said when he finished. "Where's the transporter?"

"There," Karff pointed. Overhead the low clouds were tinged with red by the lights of the city. The transporter had exactly the same luminosity, but it was a neutral gray. The untrained eye would miss it. At a greater altitude, even the trained eye would miss it without optical aids.

"I see, Colonel. You can hear the rotors, but you almost can't see it, can you?"

"That's the idea. Something that big and that slow needs all the help it can get."

At the foot of the loading platform someone had ignited flares. They burned lurid red in the gloom. Overhead, the transporter switched on its landing lights, and slowly swung around toward the flares. Waiting were flatbed trucks loaded with containers, and a detachment of military police standing behind a black-and-yellow-striped traffic barrier. A murmur ran through the crowd, and individuals began moving down the ramp. The MPs waved them off.

Colonel Karff strode up to the barricade, Detana behind him.

"You can go through, sir," the MP said, "but the civilians have to stay over there."

"Let me talk to your superior officer." Presently Karff found himself confronting a paunchy exbartender type wearing a major's insignia.

"I'm sorry, sir, but my orders are to load the containers first." He fumbled a pink piece of paper from his pocket. "See? General Bloyer signed it himself. That there's his household effects. Furniture and like that. It has priority. Anybody gets bumped, they can take the next transporter, right?"

"Wrong," Karff said coldly. "This is the last one." The scrapings from the bottom of the barrel, he thought, looking at the major. I wonder where they found him.

10

"Oh." The major rubbed his nose uneasily. "I don't know about that."

"I do. We also suspect that General Bloyer is a traitor. Load the people first, or I'll arrest you for treason and have you summarily shot." The major looked at Karff, and then at Detana, standing with his machine gun at port arms.

"But—but the general's furniture?"

"Is a traitor's furniture worth dying for?"

The major swallowed with difficulty. "No, sir."

"Very good," Karff said pleasantly. "Excellent. We seem to be in complete agreement." He turned to Detana. "Get 'em on board!" As Detana took down the barrier and waved the refugees onto the transporter, Karff turned back to the major.

"Would you like to join us?"

"Oh, God, *no!*" said the major. "Portales is my home."

Karff smiled. "What will you do now? Surrender?"

The major shook his head. "No, sir. Fight to the bitter end, sir." He might not be bright, but he wasn't going to tell a secret police officer that he was about to desert.

"Very good, Major," Karff said softly. "Carry on." He walked past the barricade and climbed into the transporter at the very end of the line. A warrant officer met him at the top of the ladder.

"You're the senior officer, sir?"

"Yes, ma'am." He removed his black gloves.

"Is that all?"

Karff didn't even look back. "That's the lot, ma'am."

The ladder retracted and the door sealed itself behind it. Then, like some great beast relieving itself, came a flood of water as the transporter dropped several tons of ballast. Slowly the transporter rose, swinging ponderously into the wind, and with a roar of rotors it began to climb laboriously toward the clouds above.

A dirigible, even a sophisticated buoyant lifting body such as the transporter, cannot reasonably expect to get off a planet without help. Once above the clouds and the turbulent lower air, help arrived in the form of a tractor beam, and the transporter was moved swiftly into space.

There it was berthed on the IMT *3261*, a transporter carrier, and the Imperial Fleet, what was left of it, formed into a convoy. After each ship was precisely aligned in formation and the whole firmly held in place by mutually supporting tractor beams, the convoy went into *i*-drive.

In his classic work on mechanically simulated telekinesis, *MST Praxis*, Nimzovitch says, "A curious thing: a tractor beam is nothing but the laser that monitors the position, velocity, and direction of the object being acted upon. This information enables a Far Action Device (FAD) to apply force at a distance by means of mechanically simulated telekinesis. Without this information, the FAD does not work.

"Since the *i*-drive is used for faster-than-light travel, ships in *i*-drive should not be able to travel in convoys held together with 'tractor beams,' which are physically dependent on beams of light. However, it is a fact that they do. It is also a fact that if the tractor beam is interrupted or turned off it cannot be reestablished in *i*-space. None of the theories addressing these points is particularly satisfactory, and some of them are positively mystical."

Chapter 2.
Journey into Darkness

GENERAL FRANCISCO BLOYER sat at his computer, trying to reconcile assorted genealogical charts with various proposed tables of organization for the Imperial Household, now crammed into the battleship ISS *Grand Duke Grossnickel*. There was a knock at his door, and he checked himself in the mirror.

"Come in," he said, and his executive officer, Lieutenant Colonel Schrader, entered. "Good morning, Sir. I have the data on Malusia."

"Let's hear it, Schrader. Not the numbers—give me the translation."

"Yes, sir. Malusia is the minor member of a binary planetary system. The major member is Aqua Pura. About one point-four Earth masses. Extensive hydrosphere, atmosphere is mostly hydrogen and water vapor. Surface pressure is forty-five hundred millibars."

"So?"

"So it's small enough and hot enough to be losing hydrogen, although very slowly. Which means that the residue is enriched in deuterium. Which we are going to need."

"Yes," Bloyer said. "I'll remember. What about Malusia?"

"It's near Earth-normal. As a moon, Aqua Pura has a period about eleven months long . . . about eleven-twelfths of the solar period. The tides are one hundred nine percent of Earth-normal, but the periods are different. From Malusia, Aqua Pura subtends an angle about one-half that of Luna as seen from Earth. So it has about one-fourth the total area. On the other hand, Aqua Pura's albedo is about six times that of Luna, so it's one and a half times as bright."

"Stop showing off your mathematical dexterity, Schrader," Bloyer growled. "What about *Malusia*?"

"It's being terraformed. They started maybe nine centuries ago, and that's about all we have."

"Then that will have to do, won't it?" Bloyer sat back and cracked his knuckles. "Was there anything else?"

"A staffing anomaly, sir. You put Colonel Himmelreich in charge of security on Transporter Carrier IMT *3261*, and Senior Colonel Karff is on that same ship. He really ought to have the job."

"Karff isn't a team player."

"Himmelreich is totally useless, sir."

"Now, now, Schrader, we all have our little faults."

"Yes, sir. On IMT *3261*, Ring 5, Karff had his group shaken down for weapons and moved into their billets before Himmelreich got off the mark on Ring 1, and Himmelreich had a full day's head start. Can you afford to keep him?"

"I know him. We were at the academy together. Where the hell did Karff come from?"

"I'd have to look it up, General, but he was doing a good job for us."

"No doubt. But he isn't a team player. He can take care of Ring 5 until we need him."

When Karff conducted the shakedown in the Ring 5 barracks, he acquired a mistress with green eyes and long red hair.

Her name was Elise Luise Obriano, the principal mistress of the late Minister of the Interior, and she had come to Checkpoint Tango in a panic after a raiding group forced its way into her apartment building. She didn't pack, taking only a full-length sable coat and a handful of necklaces, jewelry worth a substantial fortune, but only a small fraction of her collection. She was reluctant to sleep in the barracks because she was afraid that what she had would be stolen. When she explained her problem to Karff, he suggested a temporary arrangement which had at least the possibility of being mutually satisfactory.

Miss Obriano sat up on the massage table and slipped a rough white terry-cloth robe over her smooth white body. The low-wattage red bulbs Karff was using in his bedroom made her hair look black.

"You are very good at massage, my Colonel. Where did you learn it?"

"On Hammerschlag." He wiped the oil from his hands.

"Many years ago. I was just out of the police academy, and they assigned me to the Department of Public Morality, otherwise known as the vice squad. I was on the detail for nearly a year, and I posed as a masseur."

"You were on the vice squad?"

"No, I was *investigating* the vice squad. When I turned in my report, there were nine indictments, six convictions, one suicide. Plus I don't know how many APs."

"What are APs?"

"Administrative punishments. Demotions, transfers, letters of reprimand. The Prince of Hammerschlag didn't like it—his nephew was the suicide—but there wasn't anything he could do about it. Officially. After the trial, I took a lateral transfer out of the system to Forlis. Want to learn a profession, Elise?"

"Police work?"

"No, massage. I'd teach you, but your hands aren't strong enough. You'd have to exercise them."

She jumped off the massage table and helped him fold it up. "That might be fun. I'm *doing* exercise, you know. Judith—Mrs. Judge Azzaro—used to be in one of the Imperial Ballet companies, and she's giving me ballet lessons. Maybe I could do hand exercises, too. Would you like to massage her whole class?"

"Not without consulting the teacher. Is she Saloman Azzaro's wife?" Elise nodded. "I knew him professionally. They called him 'Hangman,' but not to his face. Maybe I'll stop by to pay my respects."

"You'd like her, I think, Thibalt. She's old, but very fierce." She giggled. "And you just did. Massage her whole class. It's *me!*"

"That's nice." Karff reached for the light switch. "Now climb into bed."

Later, as she lay in his arms, debating whether to bite the shoulder or attempt the earlobe, she sensed that he was going to sleep. "Malusia," she said softly, "where is that?"

"Eh?" he murmured. "Ninety-four days away. Ninety-one, now."

"That's how far it is," she said, blowing at his ear. "*Where* is it?"

He shook his head. "I don't know the vectors. You know where Portales is?"

"On the very edge of the Empire. We learn that in school."

"Right." Karff yawned. "Malusia is as far away from the Empire as you can get in ninety-four days. One lonely planet in the middle of all those unfruited stars." He yawned again.

"What are we going to do when we get there, Thibalt?" No answer. She bit him on the shoulder.

"I don't know," he said. "Now go to sleep."

On the seventh day out of Portales, Judge Saloman Azzaro hanged himself.

A judge, even in exile, remains pillar of the regime and is entitled to a certain minimum respect. Thus the Chief of Security on the IMT *3261*, Colonel Himmelreich, visited Ring 5 to oversee the investigation.

While his field officers were out conducting interviews and filling in the proper forms, Colonel Himmelreich, a tall man with wavy blond hair, made himself comfortable in Karff's office. "Well," he said, after Karff had asked the charge of quarters to send up coffee, "suppose we get started." He opened his crested attaché case and removed a small printing recorder, set up the main microphone, and removed two smaller microphones, which he checked out. Both worked. He clipped one to his tunic and handed the second to Karff.

"Print date and time," he said. "Place is Ring Five, Office of Colonel S.T. Karff. Present are Colonel Karff and Colonel Himmelreich."

"Senior Colonel Karff," Karff remarked. "What is it that you want?"

"I thought perhaps you might give me an informal statement of your findings. Nothing definitive right now, of course."

"You asked me not to conduct any investigation," Karff said, "and so, of course, I didn't. However, I was involved with Judge Azzaro immediately before his suicide. Perhaps you would prefer to have one of your field officers conduct the interview?"

"No, no." Himmelreich looked slightly bothered. Things had started to go off track. "Just tell me what happened."

"The Azzaros had a domestic quarrel of some sort." Karff sat back in his desk chair and put his feet up. "At one point Judge Azzaro said his wife was going to leave him. In any event, he came to my office to check out the pistol we'd taken from him at the shakedown."

"Did you give it to him?" Himmelreich asked.

What a question, thought Karff. The only thing that saves him from being pretty stupid is that he doesn't have much of a chin. "Of course not," he said smoothly. "We had an argument about it. That is, *he* got very excited. He laid a court order on me, signed and sealed before my very eyes with the Great Seal of the Ninth Imperial Appeals Court on Portales. I told him what he could do with it. He then offered me a bribe, an envelope full of Reichsbank Imperiales. I told him that I wouldn't permit civilians to perform *ad hoc* executions in my jurisdiction, and he cited the Anti-Terrorist Corps as a precedent. I told him that the ATC was the equivalent of gangrene on the body politic, that—well, *you* know."

"Right," Himmelreich nodded. "This is the IMT *3261*, not Portales."

"Exactly. No viable state surrenders the authority to kill to a gang of thugs and fanatics. The whole argument. He offered me another envelope of money. It took me some time, but I finally convinced him it was worthless."

Elise Obriano walked in with the coffees they had ordered and left them on Karff's desk.

"How did you do that?" Himmelreich asked, reaching over for his cup.

"With logic and sweet reason. In the end I tore the money in little pieces and threw it in the wastebasket. He got very upset and stormed out, leaving his hand seal on my desk. I sent it back to him by runner, and about an hour later the runner reported back that Judge Azzaro had hanged himself."

Himmelreich sipped his coffee. "What took him so long— the runner, I mean."

"He had a list of errands. When we went over, we found the judge hanging by an electric cord. On the floor were millions and millions of Imperiales. Two suitcases full. He must have scattered them in a frenzy and then hung himself."

"He took paper money? Incredible." He sat back in the leather easy chair. "Why did his wife leave him? Not that I blame her."

Karff took a drink of coffee. "She didn't want to come with him. He told me that he had brought her on board at gunpoint."

"What about his estate?"

Karff walked over to a storage cabinet and opened it. He took out two large suitcases, a pistol with a tag, the Great Seal of the IXth Imperial Appeals Court on Portales, and two cigar boxes. The cigar boxes he set on the desk and opened for Himmelreich. One was full of plastic ROM cases, the judge's law library. The other held two cigars.

Himmelreich took one cigar, Karff took the other, and they lit up.

"That's the lot?" said Himmelreich blowing smoke. "What about the money?"

"It was swept up and thrown out."

Himmelreich nodded and put away his recorder. He gave the transcription to Karff, who read it, made a few corrections, and signed it.

Himmelreich blew a smoke ring. "Usually, you know, it's the lawyers who wind up smoking the soldier's cigars."

Which are you? Karff wondered.

"By the way," Himmelreich added, "who was that redhead who brought in the coffee?"

"Miss Obriano. Is there anything else?"

"I can't think of anything."

When the field officers reported to Karff's office with Mrs. Azzaro, Himmelreich had finished his cigar and was ready to return to Ring 1. "Accept my condolences on the death of your husband," he said, clicking his heels and bowing like a courtier. "We have no further questions at this time." He and his field officers left without ceremony.

"We haven't met, Mrs. Azzaro." Karff offered his hand. "I am Senior Colonel Karff."

"I'm pleased to meet you," she said, shaking his hand. "I *was* Mrs. Azzaro, but I was born Rakoczy, and I shall be Judith Rakoczy from here on out."

"I'm pleased to meet you, Judith Rakoczy," Karff said. "Elise Obriano has told me about you." From what Elise had said, Karff expected an old and fierce ballerina, complete with tutu and toe shoes. Judith was a tall and shapely woman of perhaps forty, dressed in a red velour shirt and black slacks. The only suggestion of the ballet was her light brown hair, which she wore in a dancer's knot.

18

"I don't suppose your late husband had any more cigars around," he added wistfully.

"No, but you'll probably be able to pick some up on Malusia."

"Oh?" Karff's eyebrows rose slightly. "Why do you think that?"

"Malusia was founded as a Mamnu colony six or seven hundred years ago, and we *always* cultivated tobacco."

Karff took her by the elbow. "Please be seated," he said, guiding her to the leather easy chair. He loomed over her for a second. I should offer her coffee, he thought, but I don't want Elise bringing it in. "You're the first person I've met who knows *anything* about Malusia." He sat down behind his desk and leaned forward. "You've aroused my professional interest, Judith. How do *you* happen to know about Malusia?"

"My mother was Mamnuish," she answered, "and her mother saw to it that I learned the language and our history. The religion, too, although that didn't take."

"Ah," Karff mused, "the secret heart of the culture. You were saying?"

"The Mamnu colonized Malusia from Portales shortly before Portales itself was conquered," she said. "We'd colonized Portales originally, but the dominant culture writes us out of the histories." Judith smiled. "*Your* Empire isn't the first by a long shot, you know."

Karff folded his hands and studied her for a moment. "How well do you speak Mamnuish?" he asked. "Could you teach it to me?"

"I was fluent when I was younger. I could *try*, if you want."

"We can at least look into the matter," he said. "When we reach Malusia it might be useful."

Lieutenant Colonel Schrader turned from the files and picked up the intercom on his desk at the third ring.

"What is it, Herr General?"

"Where are the paintings?" Bloyer asked.

"What paintings, sir?"

"The Schluderberg Collection. The royal family had it on loan to the National Museum, Schrader, and I promised to bring it out for them. Count Franz-Otto just asked me about it."

"*Those* paintings. We don't have them, sir."

"*Imbecile*! Why the hell not?"

Schrader consulted his yellow notebook. "They were packed up and sent to Checkpoint Tango in time to make the last flight off Portales, sir." Schrader keyed in a reference. "They appear to have been displaced." There was a long silence.

"I can't tell Franz-Otto that," Boyer said at last. "What happened?"

"We'd packed them as your personal furniture, and it came down to the choice between your furniture and three or four hundred refugees. Sir."

"Damn and blast—Who did it?"

Schrader came into his office half an hour later. "Sir, the Schluderberg Collection was bumped off the transporter by Senior Colonel Karff."

"That's *treason*. How did he *dare*?"

"The paintings were identified as *your* personal furniture, sir. The report on the incident said that he 'didn't think a traitor's furniture was worth dying for.'"

"The departure from Portales was a bad time for all of us. Has he repeated the charge?"

"No, sir. I would have heard."

"I suppose so . . ." Bloyer muttered, biting his thumbnail. "Do you think he knows anything?"

"No. If he did, he would have spoken out."

"But he suspects. And he was in a position to know."

"As long as he keeps his mouth shut, sir, it don't make no never mind."

"That's easy for *you* to say, Schrader." Agitated, Bloyer stood up, "God! There isn't room in here to swing a cat!"

"Yes, sir."

"Oh, hell." There was a long pause. "Have the son of a bitch watched."

"Yes, sir. I'm sure Himmelreich will give his usual sterling performance."

"Don't try to be funny, Schrader. I want him *watched*. And see if you can find a nice *quiet* way to get rid of him."

"You mean *discreet*, sir?"

"You know what I mean, goddamnit. Keep your eyes open for an opportunity."

* * *

At one time, perhaps seventy years before, IMT *3261*, Ring 5, had billeted the 164th Infantry Regiment from Schwabach. The regiment and its brothers went out one fine morning and never returned, and IMT *3261*, which was old even then, was simply sealed and put in storage.

Senior Colonel Karff set up his office in regimental head-quarters, a glass-enclosed room overlooking the regimental street. In the center of the room was a glass-topped mahogany table with elaborately carved and gilded legs, ending in gilt bronze talons clutching a crystal ball. Under the glass was a carved and polychromed regimental seal. Against the wall the blue, white, and gold of the Imperial standard and the red, yellow, and black banner of Schwabach framed a huge portrait of Emperor Maximilian III, the last Emperor but two. On the table, a tape recorder played classical music very softly.

Behind the table, Judith Rakoczy sat drilling Karff on Mam-nuish vocabulary as he went through the fluid, controlled motions of Tai Chi Chuan, a martial arts exercise from the dawn of history. "Your accent is much improved," she said, "and I am amazed at how fast you are picking up the vocabulary."

Karff finished the exercise and sat down. "I speak nine languages fluently, and I can make my way through a dozen others. That and not getting caught kept me from being thrown out of the police academy for rowdyism, hooliganism, and anti-Imperial behavior. Plus, of course, once you have the knack it isn't that hard. The music and the Tai Chi, for instance, are technique. The idea is to engage the whole body as you learn, so that the whole body helps you remember."

"But why that particular dance?" she asked.

"It's an *exercise*, but less tiring than doing pushups. The down-side of involving the body this way is that when the body says it's time to stop, you have to stop. Shall I have the charge of quarters send up some coffee?"

"That would be nice." As Karff reached for the phone, it rang.

"Warrant Officer Gray to see you, sir," the CQ said.

"Send her up," Karff said. He turned to Judith. "Break for coffee?"

"I'll bring it up," she said.

Warrant Officer Gray, an almond-eyed brunette wearing the

21

gray, white, and blue camouflage-patterned jumpsuit of the Imperial Transportation Service, entered.

"Hello, ma'am," Karff said. "Do you know Judith here?" Pamela shook her head. "Judith, this is WO/Four Pamela Gray, the copilot of the transporter we came up on. Warrant Officer Gray, this is Judith Rakoczy, my Mamnuish teacher."

"Pleased to meet you, ma'am."

"I was just going out for coffee," Judith said. "Can I bring you some?"

"Thank you, no. I'll only be a minute."

As Judith left, Pamela turned to Karff.

"Mamnuish?" she said softly. "Why would you want to learn Mamnuish, Colonel?"

"L'ennui, c'est moi."

"Speak Imperiales, please."

"'Boredom, it is I,'" he said agreeably. "Also, it would appear that Mamnuish is the language of Malusia. What can I do for you?"

"I'm hand carrying some training forms for a course we're giving on the transporter simulators. Maybe we can get our bus fully staffed for once."

"What do I do with these?" Karff asked.

"Sign them. Captain Detana and Master Sergeant Arcziari both put you down as their commanding officer."

"Boredom is the devil," he said, signing the forms. "You think this will keep them out of mischief?"

"Perhaps," she said taking the forms back. "Thank you, Colonel."

At the door she paused. "Colonel Karff, sir, this is none of my business, but I took the wrong trollyvator yesterday, and wound up at Ring One. On the platform I saw your girlfriend talking to a tall blond security colonel."

"That would be Colonel Himmelreich. Are you sure it was Obriano?"

"It was that mane of red hair that caught my eye," Pamela said, "but it was her, all right."

"Did she see you?"

"No. She got on the trollyvator with me, but she doesn't *see* women, if you know what I mean."

Karff nodded. "I wonder what she wanted?"

22

"Again, it's none of my business, Colonel, but if I were you, I'd be wondering what *Himmelreich* was after."

Half-asleep, Karff was lying with one hand resting on Elise's jasmine-scented hair when something she said stirred him in the direction of wakefulness.

"Uhnh? I wasn't listening, sweetheart."

"You're such a good person, Thibalt . . . didn't you ever do anything bad?"

Suddenly he was awake. "I have cheerfully done much evil in my lifetime," he said softly. "In the line of duty, of course." He yawned unfeignedly. "Now go to sleep."

"That isn't what I meant," she said. "Didn't you yourself ever do something that you felt was wrong?"

"Well, yes, actually . . . It was a long time ago—the summer I entered the police academy, or maybe the summer before that. I was a young hellion in those days, if you can take the word of a broken-down old fart like me . . ." He sighed and stopped talking. She turned to face him and shook his shoulder.

"Go on, Thibalt—I want to hear it."

"It must have been the summer before," Karff said. "I wasn't taking the makeup math course." Elise, he thought, you have no subtlety at all as an interrogator, and maybe less subtlety than most women. You're altogether too beautiful to be any damn good at anything. "My family was quite wealthy, and we had a big house with a walled garden and these great, old apple trees. Very fine apples they produced, too. Now, our next-door neighbor—on the other side of the wall—had pear trees in his garden. They must have produced the best pears in the whole world, and he really enjoyed them. Sometimes his wife—who was very young, almost my age, in fact— would give me one or two, so I knew how good they tasted.

"Anyway, one evening when the moon was full, I decided I wanted some of those pears more than anything else in the universe. So I got out of the swimming pool, and climbed the apple tree, and crawled along the top of the garden wall to where I could reach those wonderful pears. And I didn't have anything to carry them in, so I took off my swimming trunks and pulled the drawstring at the waist very tight, so the pears wouldn't fall out . . ." He yawned again.

"And the young wife saw you? What happened? Did she wave to you, and you not come?"

"Oh, no," Karff said. "I stuffed my trunks with pears and clambered back to my own garden, where I ate them. The most wonderful pears in the world, made even more wonderful for being stolen. I had never enjoyed anything so much, ever— maybe I still haven't, for that matter—and afterward I felt so exquisitely guilty about stealing from my neighbor. *That* is what makes it so memorable, the guilt. As crimes go, it would have to be counted as the smallest of small potatoes, and surely the statute of limitations has expired over and over again. But I never forgot it. Perhaps if I had been a better person, a more moral person, I could have been inspired to lead a saintly life. Instead I failed second-semester calculus the next year, and had to go to the police academy." He yawned again. "Maybe I could have gone to the Imperial Saint's Technical Institute if I had passed calculus—my marks in repentence were very high—but that's water over the dam..." He fell silent, and after a while he felt her relax and go to sleep.

Karff lay in the darkness beside her for a long time. *She probably has a short-range wireless mike on the lamp or the headboard,* he decided. *And somewhere in the immediate vicinity a recorder to pick up on it for rebroadcast. Or, more likely, she can just take the tape in when she has something.*

The next morning he took a flashlight and turned up a cowbug, a little recorder-receiver, taped to the underside of the bottom shelf of the utility closet in the corridor behind their bedroom, where it could be milked at leisure. He worked the tape loose and removed it from underneath the shelf.

"I'll kill the treacherous bitch!" he growled, looking at the device in his hands. Then his survival reflexes began to function. *If* someone is out to get me, he thought, killing their agent will provide a pretext to come down on me. If I don't kill her, she figures to hook up on the social ladder about as high as it goes. *Any* reprisal will make her mad at me, but do I care? I don't need unfriends in high places, he decided. Why did Himmelreich put her on to me? I haven't been bothering *him.*

He turned the cowbug over in his hands until he found the erase switch and wiped it clean.

Perhaps "treacherous" is a little strong, he decided. After

all, I didn't exactly woo her with professions of undying love. What did I expect?

When Obriano returned from her ballet lesson, he returned the jewelry she had given to him for safekeeping, and her fur coat, and sent her off to Ring One.

Chapter 3.
Malusia

ON THE EVENING of the ninety-fourth day out of Portales, the Imperial convoy dropped out of *i*-drive 1,067.5 light-seconds from Malusia and 61° 34′ 16″ above the plane of the ecliptic. Maintaining convoy formation and radio silence, the fleet moved to a low orbit above Aqua Pura at constant acceleration/deacceleration of 980 centimeters/second/second. It arrived 5.9 days later.

At Aqua Pura the fleet took on deuterium to replenish the fuel for the hydrogen-fusion power plants. A drogue was trailed in the upper atmosphere by means of a tractor beam. The gas scooped in was passed over a heated palladium foil that diffused out 99.99 percent of the H:H and 99.90 percent of the H:D, enriching the deuterium from 0.4 percent to 4.0 percent in the gas that was retained. This gas was then reacted with a magnesium alloy in a replaceable cartridge and returned to the ship as magnesium hydride/deuteride. On the ship the cartridge was stripped of hydrogen/deuterium and recycled. The process gas was refined, and the hydrogen was discarded.

On the ninety-seventh day after leaving Portales, immediately after turnover, Karff placed a phone call to General Francisco Bloyer.

"What do you want, Colonel?" Bloyer asked when he eventually got on the phone.

"Sir," Karff said politely, "some of the pictures taken on the way in are quite suggestive and ought to be investigated further."

"Possibly. Possibly so. However, the Imperial Household has decided that they cannot risk losing a ship . . . the cruiser ISS *Schutzhelm* was under consideration . . . in order to make such an investigation at this time."

"I understand, sir. It would not, however, be necessary. There is ample FAD capacity on the IMT *3261* to handle a transporter as a manned photographic drone."

"Are you making a formal proposal, Colonel Karff?"

"Yes, sir. Transporter *42210*, gross weight 81.7 tons, is standing by. We have telescopic TV cameras mounted in the canards."

Bloyer grunted. "How many people on board?"

"A crew of four, Captain Julia J. Ildenhagen commanding."

"A *captain*?"

"In the Transportation Service."

"I see. *You* aren't going?"

"No, sir."

"This is *your* mission, Colonel Karff."

"Yes, sir. And I accept full responsibility for it."

There was a pause. "Very well, Colonel. Proceed as you see fit."

Karff hung up the phone, turned to Commodore Brodyk, captain of the IMT *3261*, and handed him the transcript of the conversation.

"There you are, Commodore," he said pleasantly, "the mission is authorized. You may proceed when ready."

Chapter 4.
Malusian Pioneer

FIVE DAYS AFTER the Imperial Fleet reached Aqua Pura, the Red Audience Room on the ISS *Grand Duke Grossnickel* was set up as a theater, and General Francisco Bloyer, Chief of Security, presented the findings of Transporter *42210* as a slide show.

"May it please the Grand Duke and the members of the Imperial Household," Bloyer said with a bow, "we feel that it is possible to draw three conclusions from the evidence that we are about to present: first, that the Malusian civilization is spacefaring; second, that the Malusian civilization does not have mechanically simulated telekinesis, the basis of contemporary military technology; third—" he hesitated, perhaps for effect, "it should be feasible to think of the conquest of Malusia"—Bloyer's notes had said "must be feasible," but one did not use the word "must" to the Imperial Household—"Malusia may well become our future homeland." There was applause at that. A homeland was sorely missed. He pushed the button on the slide projector control.

The first slide showed a group picture. Captain Julia J. Ildenhagen, pilot, and WO/4 Pamela Gray, copilot, wearing the patterned blue-gray-white jumpsuits of the Imperial Transportation Service, Captain Hans Detana, radar and navigation officer, wearing the dress blacks of Imperial Security, and Master Sergeant Rost Arcziari, engineering and loading Officer, wearing fatigues. At the extreme right stood General Bloyer, neatly superimposed over the figure of Colonel Karff. The second slide showed Transporter *42210* as seen from IMT *3261*. The transporter moved clear and reoriented itself and suddenly appeared very far away, an almost invisible spot marked with an arrow.

A space habitat appeared and grew to fill the screen.

"You will observe that we have two counterrotating cylinders butted end-to-end in a stationary collar," Bloyer pointed out. "Note that the axis of both cylinders points directly at the sun, and that the mirror array extending from the collar is a flat disc. The incident sunlight is reflected back at a sharp angle to insolate the sunward cylinder, and deflected at a gentle angle to insolate the outward cylinder. Note also that the cylinders are divided into six equal portions, three of which are glass. As the cylinder rotates, half the sunlight is used on the inside of the cylinder, and half is simply reflected back into space."

"Isn't that wasteful?" a young Countess asked.

"No, my lady. It is a very economical design for the mirror. The sunlight is free. This slide is a computer drawing of the habitat showing that each cylinder is ten kilometers in diameter and seventy-two kilometers long. The total internal area of both cylinders is estimated at about twenty-two hundred and sixty square kilometers, a figure substantially larger than modern Imperial habitats."

"Why is this, do you think, General Bloyer?" Grand Duke Sergius tugged at his long gray mustache.

"Modern Imperial habitats have been built to function in many capacities," Bloyer said. "However, it has been Imperial policy that they depend on food imported from nearby planets. In most cases, the phytotron area does not exceed two or three hundred square kilometers."

"Phytotron?" someone asked.

Bloyer had asked the same question of Schrader. "A plot of arable ground where one controls insolation—that is, the light influx—temperature, humidity, and available water. Crop yields can be sustained at maximum level."

"Very interesting," the Grand Duke said. "Does the General think we are looking at a farm, then?"

"The Grand Duke has anticipated the next few slides," Bloyer replied. A look through the different windows showed monotonous monoculture farmland. Wheat growing in space. The scene shifted to the rearward end, showing the great radiators that disposed of waste heat, and backed off until the cylinder was just eclipsing the sun and the circular mirror array filled the screen. In the area closest to the cylinder, the mirror spelled out DELOS in letters of fire, and displayed a coat of arms, as well as the mirror-image of both. Three radii ran from

29

the stationary collar to the edge of the mirror, and the camera focused on one, a docking area of some sort, linked by rail to the collar, and through the collar to both cylinders. Behind the docking area the dim crescent of a carbonaceous chondrite could be seen, a rather dark asteroid several hundred kilometers in diameter. On the surface could be seen buildings and spidery towers of white and silver, in striking contrast to the surface, a mining and refining operation of some sort. The next four slides showed exactly the same image with a clock superimposed in one corner. After 1.0, 5.0, 10.0, and 31.5 minutes there was no change; the asteroid was not rotating. Close up, the buildings seemed somewhat more grimy and used. One of the largest bore the Delian coat of arms, gules upon argent, a dragon's head, erased. A motto was spelled out in one of the Cyrillic alphabets.

"The language is archaic Mamnuish," Bloyer said, "and the translation is 'I do not forget to smash the state.' Clearly, some revolutionary's descendant has made good." There was a ripple of genuine amusement.

The next series of slides tracked an arrow-marked point of light until it manifested itself as a light-sail cargo carrier. An unmanned light-sail cargo carrier. The motorized winches controlling the trim lines, the radar and communications antennae, the solar power collector, all ran back to a white, featureless sphere. A *small*, white featureless sphere. The cargo consisted of three stacked pallets, each with four containers. The next slide showed the bill of lading on one of them. More Cyrillic characters.

"That says that the container holds 74.893 tons of Number One Hard White Wheat under one atmosphere of nitrogen," Bloyer read. "All the containers hold the same thing."

Then Malusia appeared, a beautiful blue crescent, waxing and swelling as the transporter swung around to the sunward side of it and drew closer. A circular continent with a wedge-shaped gap appeared and moved across the northern hemisphere as the planet turned. The world ocean was marked with a display of scattered white clouds, weather of the most unremarkable sort. The continent lay covered at all times by uniform low clouds, as if it were in some way making its own weather. Then the ocean side of the planet moved to one side of the screen, and an arrow appeared, marking a tiny moon.

A tiny *tethered* moon.

"Grand Duke, Lords and Ladies of the Imperial Household, what you are looking at is a space elevator. A device which until now was thought to exist only in historical romances." The moon itself was cradled in an elaborate rigging of cables and was largely obscured by construction of one sort or another. On the top, a dozen large warships waited the command to launch themselves at some adversary, and with plasma drives rather than puny, fragile light-sails. Then the camera moved down the mighty tapered cable. About a third of the way down it came to the city, an ornately textured body of white and silver and crystal, lit from within by greenish lights. Mercury vapor lamps, perhaps. Down below, on the surface of Malusia, where the cable must be anchored, were several parallel lines of white cloud, each springing from a point source.

"Cities," Bloyer said. "The cooling towers for their waste heat make clouds visible from space. And they rely on their space habitats for food."

A light-sail cargo carrier approached the tethered moon. A long boom reached out and took its cargo, replacing it with another stack of containers on pallets. The cargo carrier moved swiftly away from the sun without altering the set of its sail at all.

"We infer that the containers are empty," Bloyer said. "On photographs we have identified a dozen or more habitats, and hundreds of cargo carriers. The Malusian trade pattern is that cargo moves to the freight elevators and the cargo carrier returns empty to the habitat from which it came. Lights, please." He waited until the applause died down.

"Grand Duke, Lords and Ladies of the Imperial Household. I repeat: The Malusians are a spacefaring people, but they do not have MST, and if we choose, we can easily conquer them."

"You have made an outstanding presentation, General," the Grand Duke Sergius said formally. "This project was undertaken at your own initiative?"

"Yes, Grand Duke."

"Attend us in the chamber." Sergius rose.

Behind the Red Audience Room lay the Robing Chamber, a small room in which the Grand Duke sometimes held informal audiences.

At the door General Bloyer paused and carefully combed

his lank black hair over his bald spot. When Count Franz-Otto admitted him, the Grand Duke Sergius was wearing a green-velvet smoking jacket and sitting in a well-worn leather easy chair. His bemedaled tunic hung on a pipe rack, and he smiled as Bloyer entered. "Please be seated, General."

"I am honored, sir." Count Franz-Otto served both men coffee from a stainless steel coffeepot and stood at ease behind the Grand Duke.

"Yes," Sergius said, stirring in cream and sugar, "that was a good piece of work, your presentation." Bloyer grinned and nodded, saying nothing. "You know, of course, that we cannot hold Malusia if we take it, do you not?"

The grin faded. "I know nothing, sir. What is the difficulty?"

"The Rebel Fleet. For various reasons, which I do not choose to debate or rehearse, I believe that they will follow us here. If we are involved with Malusia, we will be unable to run. We would *never* be able to fight."

"*If* the Rebel Fleet comes," Bloyer said, "that would most assuredly be the case." He took a cautious sip of coffee. "However, with all respect due the Grand Duke, they might *not*. Permit me, sir, to outline my plan, which covers *both* cases."

"If I err, it must be on the side of caution," Sergius said, "but you have earned a hearing. Proceed, General."

To: Sr. Col. S.T. Karff
Subject: Malusian reconnaisance
From: Gen. F.L. Bloyer

I. You are hereby requested and required to prepare and conduct the subject operation at the earliest possible opportunity.

II. Transporter *42210* is assigned to your command for the subject operation and is to be staffed and outfitted as you deem appropriate to ensure the success of your mission.

III. The purpose of the subject operation is to gather information of a military, technical, and political nature that would facilitate the Imperial conquest of Malusia.

IV. You will be expected to provide a first-hand ac-

count to HIH the Grand Duke Sergius, Regent for Prince
Fredy.

/s/

General Francisco Bloyer, Chief of Security

The beautifully matted and framed portrait of the dashing
Emperor Maximilian III had been removed from its place of
honor in Karff's Ring 5 office and replaced by a poster of
Prince Fredy in all his youthful wimpitude. If Karff felt that
the substitution made any comment whatsoever on the state of
the Empire, he kept it to himself.

"What did you think of the memo, Captain?" he asked.

"We'll have to do some work on the transporter," said Captain Julia J. Ildenhagen, a small, sinewy woman who looked
like a veteran jockey with a clean shave. "We need new bearings on the main rotors. We need a new microwave generator.
The controls need work. So does the radar. You want to go
joy-riding around on a strange planet, fix up the old bus first."

"Fine," Karff said. "Make a list and get going on it. I can
give you anything except time. How long will you need?"

"Can we pull people off the other ships?" she asked.

"Yes. I'd be very surprised if we could *not*."

"Well, then, if we can get the new bearings..." she tilted
her head back and looked down her nose at him through half
closed eyes, "four, maybe five days, altogether."

"Send word that you need it in forty-eight hours," he said,
"and send it by thirteen hundred hours today. Give me a list
of who-all you went out to, and I'll follow up on it."

"They can only do what they can do, Colonel."

"Right. And I'm going to see that they do it." Karff grinned.
"The memo puts *my* ass in a sling if *they* don't perform."

Detana leaned on the glass-topped table. "Another thing—
we need someone to operate the FAD-200."

"Damn straight," Karff said. "What's a FAD-200?"

"A Far Action Device with a rating of two hundred joules,"
Detana replied. "We used it to move the small camera around
for the closeups on the cargo carrier, for instance."

"Do we need it for *this* mission?"

"It would be handy. The thing can accelerate a hundred-
kilogram body one gee against a one-gee gravitational field.

33

You could keep the transporter at a respectable altitude while you put someone down."

"Or picked the sucker up in a tearing hurry," Ildenhagen said. "You take the FAD, though, you won't be taking much else. The mother weighs in at eighty-seven hundred kilograms."

"You'd save on stored food," Pamela threw in. "With the FAD-200 you can take daily deliveries from the fleet."

"Ye-es," Ildenhagen conceded. "Or a new crewman. But you'd still want some emergency rations on hand. Freeze-dried stuff."

"I could see that," Karff said. "And we'd save on fuel the same way."

"Ah, not exactly, Colonel," Ildengagen said, covering her smile. "The transporter is, you know, solar-powered. The topside is covered with a photovoltaic film."

Karff grinned. "I knew that," he said. "It just slipped my mind. What happens at night?"

"We run on the hydrogen/oxygen fuel cells, losing a little buoyancy in the process, maybe."

"So we don't need fuel," Karff agreed. "What about the crew?"

"There's the three of us," Detana said, "and Arcziari makes four. And you make five. And we'll need someone to operate the FAD-200. Six."

"We'll need a translator for Mamnuish," Karff reminded him. "Seven."

"You speak Mamnuish, don't you, Colonel?" Detana asked.

"Not fluently. I'll need a translator's support to do a professional job. Besides, I don't want to do all the work myself."

"How long are we going to be messing around down there, Colonel?"

"I don't know, Captain. Weeks rather than days, anyway."

"Then we'll need a cook. That's eight."

"I expect you're right," Karff agreed. "What about living arrangements?"

"We have some standard layouts," Gray said. "I'll get the plans from engineering. You pick one and we can have it installed in no time."

"Good enough—Let's get moving on it."

After Ildenhagen and Gray left, Captain Detana turned back to Karff.

"A question, Colonel." He picked up Bloyer's memo.

"Yes?"

"This talks about the 'conquest of Malusia,' right? How does it square with the memo that came through two days ago saying we should refit our sewage treatment system to use anaerobic bacterial digestors?"

Karff almost laughed. "I don't make the connection," he said. "Lay it out for me, please."

"Right. Our present system runs the aqueous sludge into a hyperbaric reactor. A little acid, heat, and ozone, and a couple of atmospheres of oxygen—you come out with CO_2, clean water, and a little undigested cellulose. It works beautifully. The only thing is, for serious recycling—which is what you need for any extended trip—it's inefficient. The anaerobic digestor converts your organic carbon into CH_4 and CO_2, and you can then convert the CH_4 into methanol, which is your basic feedstock for edible bacteria."

"Single-cell protein!" Karff's distaste was evident. "That's eating about as low on the hog as you can get."

"Absodamnlutely, Colonel. But it's what you do when you take a lot of people on a long, long trip. Or hit out for parts unknown. Which is *not* charging in to take over your local backward planet. Which is what *this* memo is talking about."

"So what is your question?"

"Changing the sewage treatment system says we're going to run. Conquering Malusia says we're staying here. Which is it?"

"It could be either one," said Karff. "I imagine it depends on whether or not the Rebel Fleet comes after us."

"Yes, sir. *If* the Rebel Fleet turns up, we run. *When* it turns up. Can you possibly think that it *won't*?"

Karff shrugged and said nothing.

"Sir, when the Rebel Fleet turns up, you—*we* will be on Malusia. Two, maybe three days away. That's what Bloyer wants."

Karff grunted. "So?" he said at last.

"So the Imperial Fleet will leave within hours."

"Probably so," Karff agreed at last. "But why would he bother?"

"Sir, you've already called him a traitor before witnesses. At Checkpoint Tango."

"At the evacuation?" Karff pulled at his nose. "Nobody will remember, Detana."

"With all due respect, Colonel, Bloyer is going to scrape you off like shit from a boot!"

"You're being melodramatically cynical."

"Yes, sir."

"Good." Karff walked back to the window. "I'm glad you agree with me."

Detana took a deep breath. "Colonel, suppose Bloyer *is* a traitor?"

"He'd consider me a threat to the life, of course." There was a long pause. "Hey, Detana—" Karff turned around. "*If* he was a traitor, and *if* I knew it, and *if* he knew I knew, *then* I'd have to act." He sighed. "That isn't the way things are. Probably Bloyer is a traitor, but I can't prove it to the Imperial Household. They know *him*; I'm an outlander."

"What are you going to do?"

"Figure the odds. If I sit tight and keep my mouth shut, he's got to figure it's safer to live with me than to *try* to get rid of me. Especially if he doesn't think that I know."

"How can he *not* be a traitor?"

"If there were someone else," said Karff softly. "*Me*, for instance."

"We got delivery on the main rotor bearings," Detana announced, walking into Karff's Ring 5 office. "Arcziari sat around the shop office cleaning his fingernails with that switchblade of his, and they pushed the job through to get rid of him."

"That's nice." Karff looked up from the computer printout on the table. "We're only running a day late, then?"

"From the proposed schedule," Detana said. "What's the hurry, sir?"

"You tell me, Captain. General Bloyer has been pushing the thing." He tapped his pen on the printout. "Somewhat. This list identifies the Mamnuish linguists in the fleet. All twenty-eight of them. They aren't broken out, of course, and they are to be politely requested to volunteer. When I asked Bloyer why I couldn't *tell* them to volunteer, he shrugged and said that was the way the Grand Duke wanted it."

"Did you get any volunteers, sir?"

"Yes and no. Seven or eight officers and ratings stepped up, but none of them can speak the language as well as I can. Most of the others can read but not speak. The ones who are fluent—as, for instance, the Countess Czarski and her sixteen-year-old sister—can't see going along with the program."

"What about Judith? She's been teaching *you*, after all."

"Ye-es," Karff conceded. "She also admires my mind and the body it walks around in."

"You're complaining that nobody volunteered?"

"I told her we'd both be better off with younger lovers."

"Like Obriano?"

"Hey, Obriano is ancient history. Judith is a nice lady, but she doesn't do anything for me."

"She taught you Mamnuish."

"That's true, Captain. She *still* doesn't do anything for me. You understand?"

"Yes, sir." Detana leaned forward on the table. "What are we going to do about getting a translator? Kidnap the Countess Czarski's kid sister?"

"Draft," said Karff. "Induct. Impress, maybe. Kidnap? No. 'Kidnap' is something civilians do for frivolous reasons."

"Right," agreed Detana. "So *first* you get an audience with the Grand Duke, and *then* you tell him that his stupid idea about volunteers isn't working. And *then*—"

"Bloyer already tried that. He said."

"And?"

Karff shrugged. "Nothing. The Grand Duke did not see fit to change his mind."

"I'm sure Bloyer gave him an argument," Detana said with a perfectly straight face. "So you have maybe forty-eight hours to turn up a translator. For the good of the Empire, and the success of the mission. The Empire expects us all to make small sacrifices from time to time, now and then."

"I'm working on it."

"Making the sacrifice?"

"Finding a translator."

The next evening Karff and Detana took the trollyvator to Ring 2, where the Imperial Vaudeville and Amateur Theatric Company was holding its regular twice-weekly performance in a converted mess hall. Arriving early, Karff took a seat near the stage, and Detana ordered a carafe of white wine. The bill featured a barbershop quartet, pretty good, and tap dancers, pretty bad, and a juggler who had a nice line of patter but dropped the balls. Then Judith Rakoczy came on. She wore the classical belly dancer's costume in red and gold, decorated with jingling coins and draped with a diaphanous black veil.

She came on to a slow Theodrakis number, and as she warmed up, she saw Karff in the audience and began playing to him, and off him, and flirting with him, and as she went into high gear, she tossed him her veil. At the end, the audience gave her a standing ovation, and she gave them one encore with the finger cymbals, and a second without them.

Afterward she came out in a sweater and slacks and joined Karff and his aide at their table.

"I am impressed," Detana said. "Where did you learn belly dancing?"

"My husband made me give up ballet," she said, taking her black scarf back, "but the church offered lessons on our cultural heritage. Belly dancing was part of it, and I took it for exercise, at first. Then I began to teach it, because, you know, he never objected to my church work, my husband. Of course, I never performed in public, either."

"Fascinating," Karff said. "I have . . ."

"Yes, Thibalt?"

"I have ulterior motives," he sighed. "Look, Judith, how about sharing my bed for a six-week, all-expenses-paid tour of scenic Malusia?"

"Really?" she smiled with genuine amusement. "You want me to translate for you?"

"That too," Karff said, recklessly adhering to the truth, "but after seeing you tonight, I am aflame to possess your fair white body! And since I must leave"—he checked his watch—"in about four hours, I seize this chance to invite you along. I need you. I want you! I must have you!"

"Do you love me?"

"A good question. At the moment I can't tell whether it's love or simple infatuation."

"Are you simply infatuated with me?"

"Absolutely. You have great breasts, really *fine* breasts, and I have always been a sucker for breasts."

38

Judith laughed. "God, what a proposition. Look, Thibalt, six weeks is a long time. Where would we be living?"

Karff took out his pen and drew a long rectangle on the placemat.

"Here is the layout of the transporter. This end—" he marked off a square and rounded the corners, "—is the Bridge. Pilot and copilot *here*." He drew a couple of chairs. "Captain Ildenhagen and WO/Four Gray. You've met them, I think. On their right is this little booth for the radar and navigation officer—Captain Detana, here. On the left is the engineering officer, Master Sergeant Arcziari."

"That big *ugly* man?"

"That's him," Detana said. "He might even be the biggest and ugliest."

"Next left is the FAD operator, Sergeant Stavo. A volunteer, they said. So. Back from the Bridge is an aisle. On the right, the captain's cabin. On the left, the front entrance, and beside it, a half bath. Then cabins for the crew. Two on the right, four on the left. Then the galley and the mess. The cook is a lawyer named Schmitt. Undoubtedly a volunteer. Lawyers you always hear from. Then the aisle takes a jig. Facing front are a shower stall and a half bath. In back is my suite. An office and a bedroom with another half bath. The aisle opens out on the cargo bay deck, where they have a washer and a dryer."

"And the safety net," Detana said.

"Safety net?" Judith asked.

"The deck is *over* the cargo bay," Detana said, "and *in* the cargo bay is the FAD-200. When you open the cargo bay doors, you can raise or lower someone *with* the FAD-200, which is being operated from up front. The net allows a little margin for error, so that when you bring them in you don't drop them."

"Theoretically, Sergeant Stavo will set them down on the cargo bay deck," Karff said. "Practically, we'll see."

"It sounds very exciting," Judith said. "Six weeks?"

"We could be recalled at any time," Detana said. Karff refilled his wine glass from the carafe and said nothing.

"I'll do it! Thibalt, you lucky dog, you've swept me off my feet!"

He raised his glass. "To us," he said gallantly.

* * *

When Karff returned to his office on Ring 5, he found Ildenhagen and Arcziari supervising the dismantling and removal of his glass-topped table. "I beg your pardon, but what are you doing?"

"We're moving your table onto the transporter, Colonel," Arcziari replied.

Karff scratched his head. "Why?" he said at last.

"You said you liked it," Ildenhagen said, tilting her head back to look down her nose at him.

"Well...ye-es, I guess I did, but I thought we were tight on what we could carry."

"That actually turns out not to be the case, Colonel," she said. "The normal atmosphere—what you figure lift on—is 80 percent nitrogen and 20 percent oxygen plus traces. The average air molecular weight is 28.8 grams per mole, all right?" Karff nodded. "So. Malusia turns out to have *more* than a trace of carbon dioxide. Not 0.2 or 0.3 percent, but 3.22 percent. Which brings the average air molecular weight up to 29.3 grams per mole."

"That doesn't sound like very much," said Karff.

"Wrong." Ildenhagen shook her head. "Try 29.3 divided by 28.8 times 100. You get 101.74 percent calculated buoyancy, so we have considerable extra lift."

"Right," Karff agreed. "But why take the table?"

"It'll be in your office," she said, grinning, "right next to the cargo bay deck. If we need to dump ballast in a hurry, there it is."

"My nice table?"

"You didn't *really* like it," Ildenhagen said. "What are you doing in the office anyway?"

"I was going to meet the translator here," he said.

"Oh? Who did you get?"

"Judith Rakoczy."

"I like her." Ildenhagen was watching the carved tabletop ease out the door. "Where will she be sleeping?"

"With me," said Karff resignedly.

"Good," said Ildenhagen, grinning. "That gives us an extra room on the transporter."

In the event, that proved not to be the case. Judith came

40

aboard with a small bag of necessities and a large bag of dance costumes and moved at once into her own cabin.

General Francisco Bloyer sat in the Grand Duke Sergius' ornately decorated suite of offices on the ISS *Grand Duke Grossnickel*, drinking brandied coffee and watching the computer-enhanced image of Transporter *42210* ease slowly away from the mother ship.

"They appear to be properly oriented and clear," Count Franz-Otto said. "Did the Grand Duke wish to convey any message to the crew before their departure?"

"I don't believe so," Sergius said. "A routine scouting mission against primitive opposition hardly calls for it. How could there be any danger?"

"Not from Malusia, certainly, sir," Bloyer said. "Of course, they might be careless. Or unlucky."

Sergius stirred his coffee with a silver spoon and said nothing.

"If you wish, sir," Bloyer said unctuously, "I will call Colonel Karff on the transporter and extend your best wishes."

"Strange name, Karff," Sergius rumbled. "He isn't one of us, certainly. Where did he come from?"

"He was with that lot of refugees from Forlis, sir," Bloyer replied. "Shall I give him a call?"

"I think not. The man may be competent enough, perhaps, but he isn't a team player."

"I must agree with you, sir." Bloyer took a sip of his brandied coffee. "And, of course, he *isn't* one of *us*."

A digital countdown appeared on the corner of the television screen, and at the appointed moment the transporter accelerated at one gee toward the brilliant blue and white half-moon of Malusia. Bloyer watched until it vanished from the screen then reached for the remote control.

"With the Grand Duke's permission," he said, hesitating. And then, with the Grand Duke's silent acquiescence, he turned Karff off.

Chapter 5.
First Contact

BENEATH ITS COVER of perpetual mist, the Malusian continent was remarkably flat. Topographically it was complex, covered with a sinuous network of bays, inlets, and rills, but in very low relief. When the tides came in to flood that network, they rolled over slimy green beaches kilometers or even tens of kilometers wide. In spring and fall, the neaptide season, the high tide was marked by thousands of flat, rounded islands. In summer and winter, the springtide season, those islands vanished. Gray-green they were, and rust, and sometimes brighter colors as different species of competing algae flourished at different moments, but in the dryer spring and fall, the islands were a uniform dull green.

When the terraforming of Malusia had begun, the continent was a gigantic seamount, a few island crescents marking out an area of shallow seas in the vastly deeper world ocean. Seeded with blue-green algae, the waters of Malusia took on life, but in the shallow seas over the submerged land mass the algae thrived, and it was there that they fixed the carbon dioxide into great algal mats as free oxygen was released into the Malusian atmosphere. Slowly, slowly the algal mats built up until they were hundreds of meters thick. The continent became flush with the surface of the ocean, and the matted algae moved out beyond the edge of the continent like a slow, soft glacier pushing into the abyssal deeps.

When the Malusian settlement was initiated, the air was already breathable at 3.49 percent carbon dioxide. From their foothold in space, the Mamnu engineers and scientists built a space elevator and undertook the colonization of the planetary surface. In historic time, the carbon dioxide had fallen from 3.49 to 3.22 percent, but each year the decline was smaller as the world ocean yielded up its vast reserves of carbon dioxide to the continent-size mats of algae that were increasingly dryer and less efficient.

The Mamnu biologists introduced new forms of algae, and marsh grass to contest the beaches. On the islands that had never been immersed by algae, they planted modified cyprus and mangrove, swamp trees that reproduced asexually, to fix the carbon dioxide in the air and extend the land. Above the level of the carefully selected plankton, animal life did not exist, save only for humans, their pets, parasites, and symbiotes.

Cruising below the tenuous cloud cover at two hundred meters, the transporter crossed the watery wasteland from east to west, heading toward a source of microwave activity identified from space. Local radio and television interceptions identified it as Malusiopolis.

Karff sat on the Bridge in the engineer's chair, looking out the window.

"Hey, Colonel," Ildenhagen called, "a little excitement ahead."

"Oh?" He sat up. "I don't see anything."

"Swamp grass," she said with a grin. "Do you think you can stand it?"

"I haven't recovered from the stand of trees we saw yesterday."

"Day *before* yesterday, Colonel."

"How time flies. I suppose I could go back to working on my accent, but television is nothing but daytime soap opera. Hey—it *is* swamp grass!"

"Sure, Colonel. The horizon changes color and texture, sort of. You can tell."

"Tell me again, Ildenhagen. When do we get to Malusiopolis?"

"Same as always, Colonel—Midnight tonight."

"I wonder where they go on vacation," Karff said absently.

Slowly the landscape changed. Stands of swampgrass appeared more frequently, and scattered clumps of cyprus or mangrove. Two hours out of Malusiopolis Detana looked up from the radar screen.

"We have something," he said. "Vector two-three-two, range eight point-five kilometers."

43

"That's not all that far off our present bearing," said Karff. "Let's take a look."

Through the pallid clouds, Aqua Pura gave a ghostly, diffuse light. Arcziari set the canard-mount telescopic cameras to record, one on infrared, one computer-enhanced visible light. From the window, the landscape appeared in monotonous blacks and grays. Karff leaned over Ildenhagen's shoulder to watch the monitors. Directly ahead, in a grove of mangroves, the infrared showed a cluster of four or five hot spots. Internal combustion engines, perhaps. Visually, there was a faint orange glow, invisible without enhancement.

"About five hundred meters ahead," Detana said, "just inside the trees. We have seven pips, all sharp. Boats, maybe, or some sort of swampmobile."

"Hold up," Karff ordered. "Sergeant, we may have a chance to catch one of the locals for interrogation."

"Yes, sir!" Arcziari touched the intercom button. "Hey, Stavo! Get your ass in gear! We want the FAD going soonest!"

Sergeant Stavo came in and took over the controls for the FAD-200. "You want to haul someone on board?" he said. "Sir?"

"If we get the chance."

"Then you ought to open the cargo bay doors and have someone standing by as a reception committee on the cargo bay deck," he said. "The FAD-200 is in *good* shape."

"Cargo bay doors open," Ildenhagen announced.

Karff turned to Arcziari. "Would you stand by on the cargo bay deck, please? Ask Judith if she'll translate for you. In case we need translation."

"Yes, sir." Arcziari nodded and moved easily back through the narrow aisle.

"What sort of interrogation did you have in mind, Colonel?"

"Well, Detana, I thought we'd try to find out what they did for excitement around here."

From the dark grove there was suddenly a flicker-flash of light, followed a second later by the sounds of small-arms fire. There might have been screams; at five hundred meters it was hard to tell. On the infrared a figure emerged from the trees and ran through the swamp grass. Engines roared into life and five pairs of headlights came on, one after another. The monitors gave regrettably little detail. After the fact, they could provide great pictures, but in real time they had limited usefulness.

Karff turned to Stavo. "The runner, bring him aboard."

Abruptly the figure shot into the air.

"Got him," Stavo said.

On the cargo bay deck, Arcziari and Judith stood watching as a woman, wet, muddy, and naked, was tossed none too gently into the safety net. Judith caught her by an arm and shoulder and Arcziari grabbed her by the ankles to bring her inboard.

"Easy, honey," Judith said in Mamnuish, "things are going to be all right." She turned to Arcziari. "Bring me the first aid kit, Sergeant—can't you see she's hurt?"

Below, five hovercraft, powered with jet fans, slowly spread out, flashing searchlights.

"We have all the pictures we need," Karff said at last, and Ildenhagen took the transporter up into the low-hanging clouds.

After a short time, Arcziari extracted a stack of photographs from the printer and brought them to Karff on the transporter Bridge.

The first picture was an infrared shot of an oval hovercraft, its engine luminous amidships, and a crew of four appearing as faintly glowing blotches. The second picture was an enlargement of the engine detail, showing the trifurcated fan vents. The third picture showed the same craft by available light, a shadowy and indistinct image of grays and darker grays poised in the darkness. The fourth picture was the third picture with computer enhancement. The hovercraft was white with a dull green deck. On the side of the spray shield protecting the pilot was a device, a red heart, pierced by three swords thrust upward. Under the heart was what appeared to be a decal of some sort. Taking an illuminated magnifier, Karff examined it under 12X enlargement.

The decal was a shield, bearing clasped gauntlets, sable on or, under the name NAXOS. At the bottom was a scroll, inscribed with the motto 'A contract is sacred.' The crew wore white uniforms with white caps, and reversible zippered windbreakers, dull green on the outside, aluminum-colored on the inside. Except for the pilot, the men were bearing automatic weapons. The man at the bow was preparing to fire from a kneeling position. Karff studied the weapon with the magnifier. The butt was cradled against the right shoulder, the right hand holding the stock just forward of the curved magazine. The left elbow was braced on the left knee, and the left hand was holding the pistol grip just behind the muzzle, forefinger extended so that it did not rest on the trigger. Overall, the weapon might have been two-thirds of a meter long. The next picture was the man firing, and the one after that was a computer-enhanced close-up. Eyes closed, a spent round ejecting from the chamber, he blazed at shadows.

The intercom buzzed. "It's Judith," Pamela said. "Do you want to question the woman we picked up, or should she be put to bed?"

Karff handed the photographs to Arcziari. "Tell her I'll be right back."

"He's coming," Pamela said into the intercom, then, turning to Karff, "what course instructions, please?"

"Keep heading toward Malusiopolis," Karff said, "but hold up at the edge."

"The edge is fuzzy," Detana said. "We're already picking it up on the radar."

"So, be conservative." Karff shrugged. "You *do* have the fuzz-busters on, I take it?"

"Yes, sir."

"Carry on, then, Detana." Karff left the Bridge.

The woman with Judith was young, maybe seventeen or eighteen standard years old. Her hair was dark brown and curly, and her left eye was hazel. The right eye was swollen shut, and starting to blacken. She had a bandage on the right side of her forehead, and she was wearing one of Arcziari's T-shirts. It fell to her knees.

"Good evening," Karff said. "You look a little the worse for wear, ma'am. What happened?"

"Gee, I thought *she* had a strange accent. Where are *you* from?"

Karff pulled up a chair, reversing it to sit leaning forward on its back as he faced her. "I'll ask the questions, please. What's your name?"

Nothing.

"Look," Karff said, patiently, "I don't want to blacken your other eye. What is your name?"

"Marika Sosteris," she said sullenly. "What's yours?"

Karff glanced at Judith. "Call me Mr. Thibalt," he said. "What happened?"

She sighed. "The Boulos Group, Mr. Thibalt—see, my boyfriend is a commander in the Boulos Group, and they got a contract from Delos, so they bought some new swamp-scooters."

"What was the contract with Delos for?"

"It was, ah, to protect one of the colleges at the university— I forget which one." Karff made a note.

"Go on."

"After my boyfriend went off duty we took the swamp-scooters off for a spin, you know? And we had a little slash and splash with some Hell's Federales so we took off after them."

"Excuse me, Marika, what are 'Hell's Federales?'"

"A *gang*, mister," she said contemptuously. "Thieves, gamblers, the—you know—total dregs."

"Go on."

"We took off after them. Two boatloads of us. They led us into a Perrosi ambush. After the shooting, they took off the guys that was still alive and took turns raping I and another girl. Finally, somebody said let's go, and they pushed us towards this hole that was dug in the peat. When I saw the guys kneeling beside it, I figured, oh, shit, they're going to kill us, an' I broke loose and ran off. The last thing I remember, I heard shooting, and then I fell an' hit my head, an' I wake up here."

"How did you know they were Perrosi?"

"I saw the heart with three swords on the boat. The Boulos Group uses the skull and candle."

"Right," Karff said. "Why did the Perrosi ambush you?"

"I don't know, Mr. Thibalt. I really don't."

"The Perrosi, are they working for anyone, do you know?" She shook her head.

"They had some sort of device under the swords and heart," Karff said. "Did you see it?"

"No, Mr. Thibalt."

"Two gauntlets clasped, black on gold, I think it was," Karff said.

"That would be Naxos," she said. "Naxos and Delos have been bad friends like forever, you know?"

"I didn't know. What does Delos look like—the device, I mean?"

"A jaggedy dragon's head. A red one, on silver. It says 'Delos,' and something else I can't read. Some fossilized old slogan. When we got the contract, they gave us these little stickers to put on our swampscooters. To show our group was working."

"I see. And the Perrosi had Naxos stickers, so they were working for Naxos?"

"That's right. What's *your* group? The skull and crossbones with the wreath of oak leaves on your collar—I don't pin it."

"Pin?"

"Recognize," she said. "Who are they?" Karff fingered the silver ornament on his tunic.

"The Secret State Police," he said at last.

"Gee, Mr. Thibalt, with a name like *that*, there ain't *no*body going to hire you," Marika said. "The gangs . . . the punks that give up trying . . . call theirselves things like Hell's Federales and Burrk-Rats. But *you* ain't punks."

"Thank you," Karff said.

"You're too old."

"You are a—" Karff laughed. "Actually, you needn't concern yourself. We are already in service."

"You mean *in* service? Like you're on for good?"

"For the last twenty-odd years."

"Who with?"

"If I told you, it might make it awkward to let you go. But it isn't Delos and it isn't Naxos."

"I understand, Mr. Thibalt." She clasped her hands before her and made a rather awkward bow. "Thank-you-for-your-kindness."

Karff turned to Judith. "Taking a break wouldn't hurt. Why don't you have Schmitt bring in some coffee and rolls? I've got to figure out my next questions."

The interrogation of Marika Sosteris paused for rest shortly before dawn. Weary but unable to sleep, Karff went to the Bridge, where Sergeant Stavo was standing watch. Against the lightening sky, Malusiopolis was slowly emerging out of the low-hanging mists. Karff poured himself a cup of coffee from the thermos clipped against the wall. "Morning, Stavo. How's it going?"

"Holding position, sir."

Karff grunted and took a sip of lukewarm midwatch coffee. It was almost like drinking a cigar. Rubbing the stubble on his chin, he stood watching the view from the Bridge.

The city was not large, but the towers at its center were exuberantly textured, decorated not only with carved stone and metal panels in high relief, but also with curved and sloping skylights that seemed almost to pour down ten or twelve stories to the silent fountains that were stacked and clustered in the plazas at the base of the towers. Some of the basins sported baroque bronze statues of playful or ludicrous aspect. As the mists lifted, the roofs of the towers displayed a profusion of antennas and microwave horns, an efflorescence of communications technology.

Primitive, Karff thought. Bloyer thinks they're primitive?

To the left of the towers was a windowless blockhouse. The Kalavassos, Marika had said, the maximum security prison. To the right were churches. The deeply sculptured onion domes in blue and gold were Mamnuish Orthodox. The flatter, white dome was Reform or something.

In the distance a dark wall of glass was suddenly backlit by the rising sun to reveal itself as a huge greenhouse containing the most enormous trees. Hundreds of meters wide was that greenhouse, and kilometers long, and within it were not only single trees, but groves of trees eighty and ninety feet tall that didn't begin to crowd the roof of their domicile.

The glass wall grew out of a variegated collection of buildings set more or less flush with it. Dormitories rising in terraced steps, blocky lecture halls, laboratories finished in stone, and gymnasia finished in glass block, just as Marika had said. The library would be on the other side, but even the administration building was dwarfed by the trees in that enclosed park. The University of Malusia.

Around the central area were clusters of apartments, each cluster centered around an enclosed atrium. Then apartments without atriums. Then shanty towns, with roofs of corrugated aluminum and plastic sheeting. A gas works. An airport. No industry to speak of.

Just the university and the prison system. And the local

people living off them. And the redwood trees. At least they look like redwoods.

Karff put down his unfinished cup of coffee and went off to bed.

Breakfast, at four in the afternoon, was orange juice and oatmeal, served with a shot of scotch whiskey on the side. Karff poured the whiskey on his oatmeal and worked it in with a spoon.

"That's disgusting," Judith said from where she sat with a cup of tea. "Where did you learn *that*?"

"On Forlis," Karff replied. "Their eating habits were only marginally less gross than their politics. You should see the Haggis in session, sometime. How's the girl?"

Judith had taken Marika into her cabin and bedded her down with an air mattress on the floor.

"Still sleeping. She had a rough night."

"Let her sleep." Karff turned to Detana. "What were you saying about plugging into the local comweb?"

"That it ought to be pretty simple. They have payphones all over the place. We'll amputate one out in the boonies and find out how it works. And when we know, we'll plug in."

"Right," Karff said. "I want it done tonight. Can we set it up so I can call around from the ship?"

"Sure. We just plug a relay into the circuit, and you have a five-kilometer circle you can make calls from."

"That will do for a start. The other thing is, we're going to need some local currency."

"I could engage the locals in a friendly game of cards," Detana said.

"You could apply for a bank loan, too," Karff growled. "Your face is honest enough. No. Given the situation and terrain, it looks like *robbing* a bank is the way to go."

Detana took a sip of coffee. "That's no problem either. First we find a bank, and then we case it. A couple of RBTVs from the fleet, and casing is a piece of cake."

"Excuse me," said Judith. "RBTVs?"

"Relay Broadcasting Televisions," Karff said. "Little buggers—" he held up his thumb and forefinger. "You can put them anywhere, and it puts out this feeble signal that goes to

50

the relay. Which has to be within a few meters to pick it up. The relay amplifies the signal and passes it on to us."

"And then what?" Judith was fascinated.

"That depends on what we see," Detana said. "Is the problem the vault or the alarm system? Or getting access? When we spot the problems, we solve them, that's all."

"And once we have the cash, the only problem is finding the things to spend it on," Karff said.

Judith took a sip of tea. "*Really*, Thibalt," she said, "the military *never* has trouble spending money."

"I didn't say we'd have trouble *spending*; I said we'd have trouble finding what we wanted to spend it on."

Chapter 6.
Imperial Conquistador

From: Malusian Pioneer
Subject: Intelligence report
To: HIH the Regent (attn: Gen Bloyer)

I. After four days investigating Malusiopolis, the only metropolitan area of the Malusian so-called land mass (a continental brackish peat bog is nearer the truth), we must conclude that we are about as far from the local centers of power as it is possible to get.

II. The major primary employers are the University of Malusia (UM) and the Malusian Polytechnique Institute (MPI).

A. The UM includes the College of Military Studies and the War College. The former awards a BS in engineering and a lieutenant's certificate. *Not* a commission, only the certification that entitles one to hold a commission. The latter awards advanced degrees.

B. The MPI includes the College of Forensic Science and the College of Penal Studies. The former includes a police academy, awarding a certification, not a commission, and the latter manages the prison system. Apparently this is done on a fee basis, so much per prisoner.

C. Both the UM and MPI offer other courses of study.

III. The banking system is not locally operated. What

exists is a collection of branches derived from the central banks of the various habitats. An example would be the Interplanetary Bank of Alestos, Malusiopolis Branch. Other branches are from Corsikos, Cretos, Delos, Lesbos, Melos, Naxos, Sardos, Sicilios, and Skyros, representing most of the major habitats.

IV. It may be inferred that since both universities and prisons are classical sources of disruption, the local authorities have put them as far as possible from the centers where real power resides.

    A. It is also noted (see enclosure #1) that the local phone book lists no central government. A reflection, perhaps, of the pervasive antigovernment sentiments found at all levels of this society. (i.e., the motto of Delos— *I do not forget to smash the state*—and the name chosen by a gang of street toughs—Hell's Federales.)

    B. It is possible, in fact, that no central authority exists. However, it is certain that power exists, even if dispersed. Such power is most probably centered at Enkomi, the city *on* the space elevator, or in the cities around its base.

V. Accordingly, we propose to transfer the focus of our investigation to the space elevator, with the minimum possible disturbance on the local scene.

    I remain, as ever, your devoted and obedient servant,

    /s/

Senior Colonel S. T. Karff

Detana laid the memo on the glass-topped table in Karff's office and pushed it over to Judith. "It looks good to me, but I thought we were going to ask for authorization to rob a bank?"

"That's paragraph five," Karff said. "What do *you* think 'minimum possible disturbance on the local scene' means?"

"Not bank robbery, Colonel."

"Right. But if you were worried about it, wouldn't you try to find out what we were up to?"

"Ah . . . I suppose." Detana sat back in his chair and crossed his legs. "You think they *won't* say anything?"

"I'd bet on it. And when they don't, that's authorization."

"What if they don't *notice* it?"

Karff laughed. "Well, shame on them!"

"You don't mention Marika," Judith said.

"You didn't want her shipped off to the fleet. This way she won't go."

"Good. Did you decide what to do with her?"

"After we knock off the bank, we'll turn her loose. Why?"

"What if she doesn't want to go, Thibalt?"

"What if she doesn't? We don't owe her anything."

"We saved her life," Judith said. "You can't just turn her out."

"We can talk to her about it then. Is the memo satisfactory otherwise?"

"You didn't say anything about the redwood trees," Detana said.

"*I* thought the redwood trees were interesting. But why should I put trivia in the report?"

"A fact ought to be loved for its own sake," Detana said, "and instant redwoods eighty meters tall are *interesting*."

"But what have they to do with *any*thing?" Karff asked. "It's not like they really *were* two thousand years old and Malusia less than a thousand years into terraforming."

"They make a lovely park," Judith said.

As Aqua Pura rose over Malusiopolis, the local branch of the Interplanetary Bank of Skyros sat dark and still. Overhead, Transporter *42210* hovered silently, its bulk discreetly luminous against the moonlit haze.

Karff paced back and forth on the Bridge. "What's taking them so long?"

"Sit down and watch the monitors, Colonel," Ildenhagen said. "It hasn't been all that long." Pamela Gray sat at the engineer's console, watching the green lights. Sergeant Stavo sat with headphones at the FAD-200, waiting for instructions, seemingly relaxed.

Karff walked over and peered at the monitors. "Nothing," he said.

"So don't worry," Ildenhagen said. "Detana said it's a piece of cake."

"Waiting is the hardest work there is. At least Detana has his hands full."

Stavo looked up. "They have the vault door open. Detana says there may have been an alarm."

Karff nodded and sat down in front of the monitors.

Using the FAD-200, Stavo brought in the tools used to open the vault and circumvent the alarm system, depositing them gently on the cargo bay deck, where Judith, Marika, and Schmitt put them away.

"We have a reaction," Karff said. "A police van and two police cars are moving in without sirens or lights."

"Here comes Arcziari," Stavo called. Master Sergeant Arcziari floated up with two bags of money in each hand and three under each arm. He landed awkwardly on the cargo bay deck, and one of the bags fell into the safety net.

Below, the police van pulled up to the corner in front of the bank as the police cars pulled around to the back.

"Here comes Detana," Stavo said.

Captain Detana arrived on the cargo bay deck with five bags of money in his arms and a sixth in his teeth. He let the bag in his mouth drop and grinned. "There's another twenty bags down there," he said. "You want to pick them up, Stavo?"

A second and third police van arrived, this time with lights flashing. And now police with long flashlights and short machine guns began moving around and into the building.

"Should I go after a few more bags of money?" Stavo asked, looking up.

"No," Karff said. "If we need more, we'll come back. Shut the cargo bay doors, Captain Ildenhagen, and let's drift the hell out of here."

"What about the relays and the TV monitors?" she asked.

"Pick up the relays," he said. "The monitors are expendable."

They took the sixteen bags of money into Karff's office and laid them out on his table in a neat stack.

"Let's see what we have," he said, grabbing a bag. There was a lock on the zipper that sealed it, and a manifest behind a clear plastic window. Detana took out his wallet and selected a small pick, opening the lock easily. He handed the bag back to Karff, who unzipped it and dumped it on the floor.

Banknotes in tidy bundles, sorted by denomination. The

next bag the same. Rolls of gold coin. Stacks of plastic chips. More banknotes. Loose chips and coins. Still more banknotes.

Marika stood as if transfixed.

"Hey," Detana said, "now we can send out for pizza."

"You know what it reminds me of?" Judith asked. "When my husband hung himself. There were Reichsbank Imperiales all over the floor."

"It's true," Karff said. "The only difference is that these banknotes are still in bundles."

"You must have *millions*," Marika said in an awed voice.

"So did my late husband."

"Millions of *what*?" Schmitt asked, touching the pile with his foot.

"Dolars," Marika said.

"What's a dolar?" he asked.

"The dolar is fixed at 1.4825 dolars per gram of fine gold," Karff said. "Or 674.5 milligrams of gold per dolar." He picked up a handful of loose chips and sorted through them. "Here. A one-dolar chip issued by the Central Bank of Corsikos. The note testifies to the virtue of Liberty and the Central Bank, the little gold disc at the end says '500 mg .9999 Au pur.' The note and coin neatly sealed together in plastic."

"Pretty," Schmitt said, examining it. "But you just said a dolar was 674.5 milligrams. This has only 500."

"Come on, Schmitt, governments *always* shortchange you on coinage."

As Judith translated, Marika looked up. "Malusia doesn't *have* a government."

Karff examined the chips he was holding. "The Central Bank of Melos is five hundred milligrams to the dolar," he said. "So is Naxos and Lesbos. Here's Delos, with two hundred fifty milligrams for the *half* dolar. What *do* you have, Marika? A conspiracy of central banks?"

"We have Liberty, Mr. Thibalt."

"Sure you do. You do what *you* want, and the central banks do what *they* want, and the families that own the habitats— what do you call them, Marika?"

"The Great Holders."

"Right. The Great Holders do what *they* want, too. And no government exists to say no to any of you. Is this such a great deal for *you*?"

"What do you mean?" asked Marika.

"If we turned you loose, you'd go on the street or starve. You are at Liberty to sell your ass for little chips of plastic or die of hunger."

"But I don't pay taxes."

"And you are ill-served in consequence. Don't recite the catechism at *me*!"

"What catechism?" asked Detana, catching the single word.

"Mamnuish Orthodox," Karff replied. "Tell him, Marika, what are taxes?"

"Taxes are theft, perpetuated by the mob against the individual," she replied.

"Good enough," he said. "The human mind, now—what does it contain?"

"Both good and evil," Marika said. "Intimately mixed."

"And how is the good most likely to show itself?"

"By action taken *for* the individual *by* the individual."

"Very good, Marika. And the evil?"

"Through collective action."

"Exactly so." Karff nodded. "Now, is collective action evil?"

"Not always. At first it may seem beneficial, but in time its evil nature manifests itself."

"Was the Boulos Group engaged in collective action?"

"What?" Marika seemed baffled. "What do you mean?"

"Your boyfriend, the late Tony, was a commander in the Boulos Group. The peons took his orders, right?" She nodded. "So was he engaged in collective action?" There was a long pause.

"No, Mr. Thibalt," she said at last, "the peons were all volunteers."

"Curious," he said. "Volunteers are incapable of collective action?"

"The volunteers were acting in their own self-interest," she explained, "so what they were doing was probably good."

"Probably," he agreed, "but that wasn't what I asked you, was it?"

"Tony was not evil! He would of married me!"

"I expect he would," Karff said. "Does that answer your question, Detana?"

"Hey, Colonel—I don't speak Mamnuish."

"I'll tell you about it while we put the money away."

When they finished stacking the restuffed bags under the glass-topped table, Detana turned to Judith.

"Wait a minute," he said. "*This* stash of cash was different from the Reichsbank Imperiales your husband had. There were gold coins here!"

"So?"

"So *this* money has intrinsic value!"

"Most of it is just paper," Judith said. "Promises to pay. IOUs from strangers. Put it in a couple of suitcases—how much metal would you be able to carry for any distance? Even at two dolars a gram."

"Maybe twenty or thirty kilos," said Detana.

"Sixty thousand dolars tops," she said. "Not millions. Not even *one* million. You'd need a forklift truck to move the haul we have here if it was in gold coin."

"Maybe," he agreed, "but I think a gold-backed currency is more honest than what *we* had."

"Well," Karff said, "we'll just have to check it out, won't we?"

Late afternoon the day after the bank robbery, Schmitt was on the cargo bay deck to help Marika and Judith back on board, with packages.

"Don't drop it," Judith said, "we have shell eggs."

"Hey, no problem." Schmitt juggled the grocery bag. Marika caught the egg carton as it fell out and handed it to him. "Nice catch, kid."

"Thank you," she said in Imperiales. Then, to Judith, "What did he say?"

"He said you caught the eggs well."

"How did it go?" Schmitt asked, taking the groceries into the galley.

"Eh—" Judith said. "We rented a furnished fourth-floor walk-up. Two bedrooms, supposedly. Actually one bedroom and a den with a sleep-sofa. We had to buy our own linens and towels, though."

"It has hot water, the apartment," Marika said. "Tell him about *that*!"

"Right. The landlady made a big deal about a demand heater

for hot water. You turn on the hot water spigot, and the gas goes on, and you have hot water in about ten seconds."

"*That's* the big selling point?" Schmitt rolled his eyes. "What's the place like?"

"Lower middle class," Judith replied, "but clean."

"It's a really neat apartment!" Marika said. "They have linoleum on the floors and *every*thing!"

Judith smiled. "Marika likes it. One thing it *does* have is a back porch between the kitchen and the fire escape. A little wooden deck with a wooden rail, and some clothes lines."

"That's where Stavo picked you up?" he asked.

"Yes. We can put up a screen if we need to. For sunbathing, if they ever get any sun in this place."

"Good enough," Schmitt said. "What's *this*?"

"Oranges," Judith told him. "Don't let the warty green skin fool you. Hi, Thibalt."

"Hello, Judith, Marika," Karff said as he walked into the galley.

"Hi, Mr. Thibalt," Marika said. "We got you a set of threads. You want to try 'em on?"

Karff took the package from her and presently returned wearing permanent-press white pants with a white shirt-jacket, a white cap, and white deck shoes. In his hand he had a navy blue reversible windbreaker with an aluminum-colored lining.

"What's this?" Karff asked, holding up the windbreaker. On the center of the back on the aluminum side was a black and white skull and crossbones, surrounded by a wreath of oak leaves, a good freehand rendition of his collar insignia. Underneath was the inscription *Imperial Gestapo*.

"Judith—I am *not*, for God's sake, gestapo!"

"What means 'gestapo,' Judith?"

"It's a Rebel shitword, Marika," Karff said in Mamnuish. "Originally it was a contraction of the Ur-German *Geheimes-taatspolizei* which meant 'secret state police,' but it got loaded with evil—not weights—Judith, what's the word I want?"

"Connotations. You don't like the jacket?"

"The jacket is fine. I don't like gestapo."

"The word is in local use," Judith said. "In Malusian Mamnuish it means 'union goon' or 'hired collectivist thug'—both of which are kind of mythological creatures. *I* thought it was funny."

"You would. Union goons are mythological creatures?"

"They don't have unions," Judith said, "but they remember them. The Malusians."

"I see. Did you do the drawing?"

"No. It was Marika. The windbreaker shop had a little machine that ran it off on an appliqué."

Karff put on the windbreaker dark side out. "How do I look, Marika?"

"Really tough, Mr. Thibalt. I like it."

"Thank you. If I wore it with the skull-side out would it cause any fuss?"

"No—people would think you were just with some gang that didn't have a rep. They come and go all the time."

"A new gang doesn't cause much of a stir?" Karff asked.

"Not unless they do something. If the Imperial Gestapo took credit for the Skyros bank job, that would get you plenty of attention, I bet."

"I expect it might," Karff said. "I could wind up in the Kalavassos."

"No," she said. "The Kalavossos is—how do you say— for political prisoners. They catch you robbing a bank—" She drew her finger across her throat.

"Who is *they*?"

"Whoever the bank hired to defend it. The pictures you took of the police vans showed an ace of spades pierced with a stiletto. The Michaelis Group."

"Free-enterprise police," Judith said.

"Where are the cases tried, Marika?" Karff asked.

"What do you mean? The group doesn't try cases, they catch you, they kill you. Or beat you up. The Michaelis Group. The Boulos Group wouldn't care unless you had a price on your head."

"The Boulos Group wouldn't cooperate with another group?"

"Not unless they got paid. None of them do."

"This is a strange place," Karff said. "Imperial collectivist thug, you said?"

"Imperial *hired* collectivist thug," Judith corrected him.

"Now that I think about it," said Karff, "it *is* kind of funny."

Chapter 7.

Entering the Egg

TWO HUNDRED KILOMETERS above the surface of Aqua Pura the Imperial fleet maintained position. Not a low orbit, which would be easily observable, but a position stationary with respect to the surface, maintained by the expenditure of energy through the drive FADs. This was a classical deceptive maneuver, which might enable them to observe the arrival of the Rebel Fleet and decamp unseen.

In consequence, however, it meant that Transporter *42210*, hovering in the clouds above Malusiopolis, could communicate with the Imperial Fleet only when Aqua Pura was in the sky, and when the Imperial Fleet was on the side of Aqua Pura visible to Malusiopolis. Celestial mechanics limited communication to inconveniently placed windows of time, a situation which General Bloyer found entirely satisfactory.

He sat at ease in his high-backed chair of tooled leather and basked in the magnificence of his new office on the ISS *Grand Duke Grossnickel*. On the wall a photograph of the Regent, inscribed *To Our Beloved Francisco* gazed benignly down upon him.

"What have we got, Schrader?" General Bloyer asked genially.

"A package from Operation Malusian Pioneer. A Mamnuish–Classical American Dictionary with the request that we prepare them a Mamnuish–Imperiales/Imperiales–Mamnuish Dictionary."

"Spieslinger was bitching about having nothing to do. Send it over to his shop with a work order."

"Yes, sir. Colonel Karff encloses clippings from the *Malusiopolis Star* about assorted subjects of possible interest, plus a scurrilous pamphlet entitled *Malusiopolis: Asshole of the Universe*."

"How can you *know* it's scurrilous?" Bloyer asked.

"With a title like that, how could it *not* be, sir? He feels it would be helpful to the Intelligence Section."

"Possibly so," Bloyer conceded. "How *is* the Intelligence Section?"

"The Countess Czarski took a new lover and dropped out. Susanne, her sister, is taking her responsibility seriously and doing good work."

"The sixteen-year-old?"

"Yes, sir."

"Fascinating. A pity her enthusiasm couldn't be put to better use."

"Yes, sir. It keeps her out of mischief, the Countess said. . . . Then we have a request for *My System* and *MST Praxis* by Aaron Nimzovitch." Bloyer raised an inquiring eyebrow. "It seems Sergeant Stavo, their FAD operator, is working on an advanced degree in Mechanically Simulated Telekinesis."

"So send it along."

"Yes, sir. We also have a request from Colonel Karff that a tractor beam be made available to move Transporter *42210* from Malusiopolis to the immediate vicinity of the space elevator."

"Why?"

"It would save time. Figure that he has to travel about twenty thousand kilometers at average speed of a hundred and fifty kilometers per hour. That's what—a hundred thirty to a hundred thirty-five hours. If we move him in and out of low orbit it would be maybe two or three."

"There's no hurry," Bloyer said. "Check the schedule. Probably all the surplus FAD capacity is in for rededication, but if something is available to match one of his windows, why, put him down for it."

"I've checked already, sir," Schrader said. "Nothing is available."

"What a pity. Colonel Karff is, of course, free to move on the surface of Malusia as he sees fit. Tell him I said so."

"Excuse me, sir," Schrader said, "but I think you ought to be on record as at least *asking* about using one of the FADs."

"Whatever the hell for?"

"To cover your ass, sir. Colonel Karff is entirely capable of stepping out of the chain of command and going directly to the Grand Duke. You might not look good in the Grand Duke's eyes if you simply gave him the brush."

Bloyer grunted. "Maybe not," he conceded. "All *right*. Pick the next three or four windows and ask about moving the transporter."

"If possible," Schrader said.

"Whatever. The *last* thing I want is the Grand Duke taking an interest in Malusian Pioneer."

Seeking to get inside the egg, Karff called up the author of *Malusiopolis: Asshole of the Universe*, Nick Nikolai. Nick was a newsman, articulate, opinionated, well informed, and perennially short of cash. As long as Karff picked up the bar tab, Nick would discourse at length on any subject whatsoever.

His favorite watering place was Dimitri's Bar and Oven, across the street from the *Malusiopolis Star* Building. Dimitri served hors d'oeuvres at ingredient cost and took his profits from the bar. His clientele of editors and writers ensured that profits remained high.

Karff refilled his plastic glass from a pitcher of beer and bit into a deviled egg. "Megalomania. Why would *I* want to conquer Malusia. Really, Nick."

"A pity," the small man said. "It would serve the bastards right."

"It might make an interesting article, though."

"Everybody wants to be a writer." Nick refilled his own glass. "But that's one dumb article—I mean, who'd buy it? Nobody!"

"That didn't stop you from writing *Asshole of the Universe*," Karff said.

"Hey, that was different! That was something to do when I was drying out. Therapy, sort of. Besides, I'm *already* a writer. Are you *sure* you don't want to conquer Malusia?"

"*I'm* not a megalomaniac," Karff said, "but my boss is something else. Suppose I *did* want to conquer this stinking planet? How?"

"All *ri-ight*! First off, you can't do it from here, you understand? Moptown is a dump. A trash heap. A total loss. See, what makes this place go is the university and the jail. The way it works, the yout'—rich bastards, smart punks, whatever—they come here to go to school, to the university. They riot and schlepp around, but in the end, if they want to get back to the real world, they have to shape up. Most of them do. The ones that don't, they stay here. They wind up dead. Or in the Kalavassos. Or *working* in the Kalavassos." He took a sip of beer. "Screws. The only job worse than newspaper reporting." He pushed the bentwood chair back on the tile floor and crossed his legs. "That's the students. You'd think the professors might be a little better, maybe, a little free-thinking, right? Wrong. They are the *worst* conformists you ever laid eyes on. They suck up to the Great Holders and inform on each other and hope to go on lecture tours. They all want to take a ride *up* that big elevator and live the sweet life. They might even get hired for something. Shit! Every year a couple dozen make it and the rest—"

"How many are there?"

"What? Faculty? Last semester the university enrolled 102,500 students, with a student-teacher ratio of about ten to one. Maybe ten thousand."

"Are they tenured?"

"No. You know, *I* taught literature for a couple of years when I was taking my MA in journalism. Teachers! The only job worse than screw. At least the screw doesn't have to grade creative-writing courses."

"It's a dirty job," Karff said, "but somebody has to do it."

"Shit!" the little man scowled. "You want to conquer the dog's tail, grab hold of the dog's collar. You want to conquer Malusia, you got to take Enkomi!"

"How is the city on the space elevator like a dog collar?"

"It's the choke point. The Great Holders. What do they have? Farms. That's what they have. Up in the sky, topside the space elevator. Farms. Mines too. The thing is, you can't touch 'em. If you don't like the way the Delians are cutting up, no *way* are you going to clamber up out of Malusia and kick in the habitat windows. Shit! You have to go through Enkomi, and the bastards won't even let you on the elevator!"

"Don't worry about it," Karff said. "That's *my* problem. Why should I want to kick ass on Delos?"

"Because those scum *run* things," Nick said. "That egg you're eating. The chicken laid that egg here in Moptown, but the chicken feed was imported from outer space! Raise a fist against 'em, they cut off your bread!"

"You grow your own food," Karff said. "There are green-houses all over the place."

"Shit!" Nick took the last deviled egg. "They grow salad. Cucumbers. Tomatoes. The stuff you can't ship. Twenty years ago the Stamoulis Group put up greenhouses to grow wheat. What happened? Interest rates went up, the price of wheat went down, they went broke."

"I don't know," Karff said. "I'd hate to foreclose on a bunch of farmers with machine guns."

"They cut their losses. Machine guns don't do it defending a greenhouse."

"You need a greenhouse to grow stuff?"

"Hey, Mr. Thibalt—" Nick shook his head. "You can't *grow* anything outside. The outside ain't worth shit! What we got outside is peat bog hundreds of meters deep and rock. And we're short of rock. The seasons are cockeyed, the air is fouled with CO_2, and the Great Holders would bust your market before you ever got started. But other than *that*—"

"Yes, yes," Karff said impatiently. "What about fish?"

"The same as wheat. Imported."

"You have a world full of ocean and you import fish from outer space?"

"They're frozen," Nick said. "Besides, you can't grow them. The water is too acid or something."

"You could grow them in tanks."

"You'd never recover your startup costs."

"I see," Karff said. "You can't do a thing unless the Great Holders let you." Nick scowled and finished his beer.

"That's what I've been *telling* you," he said at last. "You can't conquer Malusia from *here*." The waiter stopped by and Karff ordered another pitcher.

"Anyway," Nick continued, "how did you figure on taking Enkomi?"

"Hey!" Karff suddenly grinned. "I have this dirigible, see? It can travel through space, *and* it's invisible!"

"Shit," Nick growled. "I had to ask."

The waiter set the pitcher of beer on the table with a plate of stuffed grape leaves.

"So before we got sidetracked," Karff continued, "you were telling me about the ambush."

Nick wiped foam from his mustache. "The ambush. Yeah.

The Perros Group and the Boulos Group have been at it again recently. As if they needed an excuse. The fella you mentioned, Commander Tony, was making a rep, an' making it in a hurry. So the Perrosi took him out. No big deal, just a little slash and splash. Things might even settle down for a bit now."

"I see," Karff said. "Strictly a local affair. So Delos and Naxos aren't at odds?"

"I didn't say *that*, exactly. They aren't fighting by proxy at the moment, but they don't see eye to eye, either. Well, *shit—* they *do*—they both want to preserve the status quo. The thing is, they can't agree how to do it."

"What's the problem?"

"The problem, Mr. Thibalt, is too many people. The *other* problem is, any solution you can think of, one way or another, the Great Holders lose control. What Naxos and Delos don't agree on is who loses control *first*."

"So they lose control," Karff said. "That was the point where you asked me was *I* going to take them over. Not me. But why not *somebody*?"

"Because nobody can get *at* them. Around the base of the elevator, Ayios Sostis is an armed camp. On top of the cable, on the asteroid that's holding the thing up, Kaloutsa Naval Station is the strongest fortress in the system, maybe in the universe. Shit, they got all the lasers and counter-missiles and battleships you could shake a stick at."

"So can't the *fleet* take over Enkomi?"

"*What* fleet, Mr. Thibalt? Each of the Great Holders has a little fleet, see, and they each send a ship or two in on a rotating basis, 'Detailed to the Confederation.' They work it so that the fleet has no solidarity with anybody except their own group. And at Ayios Sostis, they can't do a thing because they can't get up the goddamn elevator. The great Holders have both ends firmly under control, an' the bastards sit in Enkomi like spiders sucking the juices out of the whole system!"

"What you need is a wasp," Karff said. "On the other hand, maybe you're better off with the spider."

"Here's to wasps," Nick said, raising his glass.

"I'll drink to that." Karff drank. "So what else is Enkomi besides the financial center of the universe?"

"The seat of the Malusian Confederation."

"Hey, Nick—I thought you said Malusia didn't *have* a government."

"It *doesn't*. All the Confederation does is keep someone *else* from forming a government!"

"That's all?"

"Yes. The Great Holders are goddamn decadent. Delos, Naxos, all that lot, don't spend a nickel more on *anything* than they have to. The thing is, you can't get at 'em. So there is no *way* you can make a revolution to shake the bastards up. But they can get at you, all right, old buddy. They can get at *me*. A word to the *Moptown Star* an' I'm out on my ass! Shit. *I* don' care. My liver is shot. I can drink myself to death before my money runs out."

"No competition," Karff said.

"What?"

"The Malusian Confederation—it doesn't worry about defense because it doesn't have any competition. The Great Holders set up just enough government to keep a *real* government from forming, and things wound up in the hands of the central bankers. And the central bankers are family, right?"

"Yeah. The oldest son usually winds up at the central bank. Or the smartest. The Great Holdings—Delos itself, for instance—are entailed estates. What did Jules say—'Sardikos belongs to *all* our family.' The sons get certified at the university, and if they shape up—that is, if they see their own self-interest and act on it—they go into the fleet or the army. Or the Church. Do good. Feed the hungry. Clothe the naked. Run the hisp-hisp-hospitals. And preach the gospel that this is the best of all possible worlds. Some of the turkeys go for it. They think the good they do will offset the lies they tell. Somebody shows a little compassion, though, the Church won't have him. *He* might want to shake things up. Shit, the poor son of a bitch will never get out of Moptown. He can go to college *forever*, for all they care. Like Jules."

"I don't know him."

"Professor Jules Pargos-Sardikos," Nick said. "The College of History *and* the College of Economics. He knows all sorts of shit. Wanna meet him?"

"An intellectual?" Karff refilled his glass. "Not really."

Chapter 8.
Pattern for Conquest, Imperial

KARFF AND JUDITH sat waiting for Nick Nikolai at a picnic table of laminated cypress under the redwood trees of University Park.

"This is nice," she said, "the air is so fresh."

"They keep the humidity in the fifty-percent range," Karff said, "and they use ionizers, but the main thing is, they pump out the CO_2. The CO_2 level is held below point-five percent."

"I don't care," Judith said. "This is the nicest place I've seen on this whole grubby planet." Karff stared up at the cool green treetops and tried to pick out the lines of the framework supporting the glass roof, but they were lost in the diffuse light.

"It is nice."

"The only thing is, it doesn't feel *ancient*," she said. "This place feels sort of like an amusement park. An amusement park *pretending* to be ancient."

"It's getting there," he said. "The plaque said it was established nearly three hundred years ago. Even if it only takes a few months to put up a redwood, some of those babies are pretty old by now."

"They're big fat fakes, Thibalt. They slip-cast a tapered concrete core, squeegee on the cambrium layer, and call it a tree."

"Unless you want to cut 'em down for timber, I don't see that it makes a nickel's worth of difference. This is a great place."

"Yes. Only it looks greater than it is, if you know what I mean."

"It's the best that could be done," he said, then spotted his man approaching. "Hi, Nick."

Nick was wearing his white shirt-jacket open over a pale

blue turtleneck. He tipped his yachting cap to Judith and made a sweeping bow. "Shit," he said, "Mr. Thibalt can really pick 'em. Call me Nick?"

"Call me Judith," she replied.

"Judith is fine. Judith is splendid." He kissed her hand, then continued holding it. "But to get right to it, Jules has a class right now. Do you want to catch the end of it, or shall I take some of Mr. T.'s money and buy us a round from yonder vending stand?"

"Let's catch the end of the class," Karff said.

"All right, you cheap bastard."

"I have the interests of your liver at heart, Nick."

"I apologise, Mr. T, You refrain from spending your money in the name of a higher morality."

"Watch it! 'Cheap bastard' I can accept."

They passed through a revolving door into a lofty foyer decorated with the heraldic devices of the Great Holders. Boulosi fighters stood around with short machine guns, hired security for the university. One of them challenged Karff at the metal detector.

"Easy there, dad. Are you packing heat?" Karff simply opened his windbreaker to show the shoulder holster. "Right. You want to go in, you got to be peace-bonded."

"Go ahead." The guard removed his pistol and inserted a long, narrow lock in the barrel. He handed the pistol back to Karff, a numbered tag dangling from the muzzle, and hung the key up on the rack.

"There you are, dad. Who were you going to see?"

"They're with me," Nick said. The guard waved them on in.

Professor Jules Pargos-Sardikos was talking to perhaps a dozen graduate students in a small lecture room with clerestory windows and a faint smell of amines. They took seats in the rear.

"Money," Jules said, holding a piece of chalk. "How does one get it, Mr. Halah?"

"Uh . . . borrow it, or collect interest on money we already have—"

"My error," Jules said. "Money is a complicated subject. Try food instead."

"We could buy it," Mr. Halah said. "Or grow it."

"That's two. Give me two more."

"Or trade for it."

"That's a variation on buying it. You can also *steal* it, and you can *beg* for it. That is how a person gets money. How does a *government* get money? Miss Zoltan?"

"They steal it."

"The classical answer. Taxation is, by definition, theft. However, it should not shock or astonish you to learn that a government may also give value for the taxes it receives, that it also receives gifts, and that it may also create wealth—"

"Such as *what*?!" a student challenged.

"Such as the space elevator. The Malusian Confederation built it. Bonds were issued and paid off. User charges maintain it. And *are* user charges taxes? And if not, why not? That question will appear on the next quiz. Anyway, governments get money the same ways that individuals do—primary production, secondary production, forced redistribution, and voluntary redistribution—make, trade, steal, and beg. There are no other ways. The difference is that governments are inefficient at making, trading, and begging, except from other governments, so they have to steal." The bell rang. "Governments are not simple things, and if you believe that government is a conspiracy against the people, you ought also to remember that it isn't the only one. The assignment for Monday is chapter sixteen in Stathis. Class dismissed."

After the students departed, Nick introduced them, and Dr. Jules, as he liked to be called, escorted them down the hall to a small faculty lounge done in green and cream. It had comfortable, shabby easy chairs and a vending machine, and on the wall were several posters advertising cigars, cigarettes, and pipe tobacco. From the typeface and costumes, Karff placed them as from the last century.

"Tobacco?" he said.

"A vegetable material," Jules said. "They don't sell it anymore. The crowning achievement of the '92 Reform Movement was banning tobacco. The Great Holders didn't reform, but they agreed that tobacco was an unhealthy weed, so to keep the peace, they stopped growing it. Now we have to find other ways to kill ourselves." He smiled and shrugged. "I'd buy a round from the machine, but I'm a little short."

"But you're a *Sardikos*," Nick exclaimed.

"The family solicitors are slow pay," Jules replied. "It's a tradition."

Karff reached into his pocket and took out a handful of plastic chips. "Kindly permit me . . ." He examined the vending machine. "They have that wine made from cheese-process waste, in two flavors, and three kinds of mixed drink. The fortified alginate slurry with candied fruit peel, the one you have to set on fire to kill the smell of, and the thing with the enormous pickled fish egg."

"Why don't you call them by their right names Thibalt?" Judith asked. "Advertising adds a little poetry, a little beauty, to our otherwise austere and—ah, unappetizing lives."

"Ah yes . . . Would you prefer Rosé Gruyere, the Chablis Gorgonzola, a Taste of Liberty, The Old Man of the Sea, or a martini?"

"Actually, Nick and I were going over to the main library. I believe I'll pass for now." Judith smiled.

"Nick?"

"It pains me to decline a free drink, but I promised to show Judith around the stacks. Hey—stay away from the canned martini. Pappas and Pappas use condemned czad roe!"

"I hadn't heard," Jules said. "Perhaps a Taste of Liberty, then." Karff brought over two cans and decanted the quivering green jelly into little plastic glasses. Slowly.

"The trick is to hit the can a few times first," Nick said after the second can had been emptied. "The drink is thixotropic, and after a few hits it will pour like water."

"Thanks, Nick." Karff handed Jules his drink. "Weren't you about to leave?" Nick smiled and offered Judith his arm as they left the room.

Jules raised his drink and Karff touched it.

"You seem to view government in a relatively positive light, Jules." Karff took a tentative sip.

"Routine antiestablishmentarianism," Jules replied, and when Karff looked baffled he expanded. "I'm against the Great Holders and the banks—the so-called establishment. So I say nice things about government in the abstract to annoy them. As long as I don't get specific, they put up with it."

"Nick says you are a dangerous thinker."

"A tautology. On Malusia, to be dangerous, one has to think. Conversely, if one thinks, one has to be dangerous."

To whom, I wonder, thought Karff, and how much. "Indeed?" he murmured. "Nick was explaining how hopeless it all was."

"Ah, Nick . . ." Jules dismissed him with a wave of the hand. "His *Asshole of the Universe* is one long whine of rage. The asshole is as necessary to one's health as the mouth, and one puts one's foot in it less often."

Karff laughed politely. "Highly amusing," he said. "Tell me a dangerous thought."

"Governments are rational."

Karff took a sip of his green slime. Either he doesn't know any dangerous thoughts or he doesn't want to tell *me*. I'll play along with him and see what turns up. "Liberal delusion. Governments tend *not* to be rational, except very new governments that don't know any better. Rationality is what gave tyranny a bad name."

"Not so, Mr. Thibalt. Originally *tyrant* meant only 'new ruler,' and being closer to the margin, a new ruler does what he must."

"Which is to act rationally under the spur of necessity."

Jules sat back and crossed his legs. "Rationality comes in many guises. In a tyranny, with its short time frame, it comes close to the popular idea of rationality. In the older regime, in the mature state, the calculus of rationality is in the service of maintaining the status quo. It is cheaper to permit a little craziness than to force matters to their logical conclusion."

"In the short run, yes," Karff agreed. "In the long run you have to pay."

"In the long run we are all dead, Mr. Thibalt, and need not worry about payment. I am, perhaps, a little more tolerant of craziness than I should be, but—is a forest rational?"

Karff looked blank. Nick did this, he thought. The son of a bitch set me up for a goddamn joke! I ask for a class-act maker of revolutions, and he turns me onto this—this wimp of academia, this theoretical fruitcake, this nerd nattering nonsense! And I can't leave until Judith gets back. *Shee-it!* He sighed. "I beg your pardon?"

"Is a forest rational? It grows and grows until it is choked with underbrush, until it is full of dead trees, until it is a mass of kindling. Until it catches fire and burns down. Surely a rational forest could tell its trees, 'Don't grow so much.' It could tell its underbrush, 'Be neater, not so tangled.' Being rational, could it regulate its growth so it would *never* burn down?"

"No," Karff said wearily, "trees must grow or die."

"Exactly so, Mr. Thibalt! Each tree pursues its own interest, growing, growing, growing. And the forest can't make them stop. But being rational, what it *has* done is learn to survive forest fires! The forest cooperates with the inevitable."

"Fascinating," Karff murmured politely. "And what has this to do with government?"

"Why, by analogy I was about to prove that government was rational. And since rationality is a good thing, therefore, *government* is a good thing. The whole argument is worth maybe a third of your final grade."

"Not *my* grade, Professor. If you like government so much, why don't you have one?"

"The Great Holders won't permit it. The function of their minarchy is to see that it never happens."

"Minarchy?"

"You need a de facto government to prevent the formation of a government. Minarchy is rule of the minimum, and also rule by threats and warnings, minatory rule. Stabilized anarchy, if you like."

Karff walked over to the vending machine and bought another Taste of Liberty. "Nick was telling me about that," he said as he hit the can. "What seems to be the problem?"

"There are lots of problems, Mr. Thibalt, and they all tie into each other. The thing bringing matters to a head is that the space elevator is running at or above its design limit."

Karff hit the can again. "So build another one."

"We—that is, the Great Holders—can't afford to."

"Suit yourself." Karff opened his drink. It flowed like water into his cup. "In that case, Malusia has to grow its own food. Right?"

"The minarchy of the Great Holders won't permit it."

"Why not, Professor?"

"Because if Malusia could grow its own food, it could form its own government, Mr. Thibalt. And the minarchy's reason for being is to prevent that very thing." He shrugged. "You see, Malusia was opened to serve as a sink for the surplus population from the habitats. And the way the Great Holders

73

kept control was economically. The shipments of food—well, if taxes are theft, the shipments of food are blackmail. The Great Holders feed the people of Malusia so they don't organize a government." Karff looked puzzled. "The Great Holders feed the people so they won't feed themselves," Jules explained. "Because *if* they could feed themselves, *then* they would inevitably organize a government."

"What's *that* worth on somebody's paper?"

"A trip to the Kalavassos. It isn't formally taught."

Karff sipped green slime. "Go on," he said at last.

"That's it. The minarchy rigs the market so we—the Malusians—can't afford to grow food when the elevator is running. And when the elevator *stops* running . . ."

"And when the elevator stops running?" Karff prompted.

"There isn't time to grow food. We starve."

"What are you doing about it?"

"Trying to underraise a government. A government could grow food even if it was losing money doing it."

Maybe I've underestimated you, thought Karff. "What kind of a government did you have in mind? A monarchy? A republic? A bureaucratic despotism?"

Professor Jules Pargos-Sardikos waved his hand in a dismissive gesture. "Just—you know, a *government*. I've spoken in favor of one for years and years. Everybody knows it. Perhaps they would look to me to lead them. If they did—" he squared his narrow shoulders, "I would form a *just* government!"

Karff almost choked on his drink.

"Taking it all off is vulgar," Judith said. "Not to mention tasteless, stupid, and cheap. It doesn't *pay*, darling."

"Ten dollars a night plus tips at the Enkomi Club isn't so bad," Marika said, resetting the borrowed belly dancing costume about her hips.

"You want to be a whore, why bother to dance at all?" Judith asked. She pressed the rewind button on the tape deck. "We'll take it from the top again. And this time don't remove even the bra. And remember, the hip motion comes from the knees."

When Karff walked up four flights of stairs to the apartment he found both Judith and Marika in costume. The music in the living room was very soft, but Marika was wearing headphones. Clearly the music was pulsing in her blood. She did two circles around Karff, letting him feel the beaded fringe of her costume brush his thighs, and on the third pass she removed her bra and draped it over his neck.

Judith turned off the music. "That will do for now," she said. "Get dressed so you can bring in supper."

Marika made a deep curtsey to Karff and flounced out of the room.

"You *said* you might do better with a younger mistress," Judith remarked with a touch of asperity.

Karff handed over the softly jingling bra and shook his head. "Not Marika."

"They're either too old or too young, eh?"

"No. Marika is terribly impressed with that stash from the bank job. She can't help it, but she is flat-out mercenary."

"It's part of the cultural milieu."

"I know," Karff said. "Malusia is about as materialistic as they come. Maybe because the people are closer to the margin. And the entertainment is pure escapism. Bureaucratic horror-drama when they don't have any bureaucrats."

"They have a lot of good material," Judith said. "The day-time soaps are pretty raunchy."

"I know. And the Church denounces the evils of collective action, unions and government alike. And nobody seems to notice that it has no relationship to the real world. On the way home a couple of Perrosi tried to sign me up for their police protection plan."

"Oh?" Judith raised an eyebrow. "The neighborhood has a contract with the Boulos Group."

"One of them offered to help me with my wallet while the other pushed a knife in my ribs." Karff reached into his pants pocket and produced a switchblade knife displaying a little heart pierced by three swords. He pressed the button, and it snapped open to show a seventeen-centimeter blade polished to a mirror finish. "This knife." He unlocked it, folded it up, and put it away. "I have a black belt in aikido and karate—and you know, this was the first time I ever used either of them in real life."

"Why take them, then?"

"For conditioning. Mental as much as physical. It makes you shock resistant. You'll never guess what my first thought

75

was when I heard the knife open." He grinned and removed
his pistol from its shoulder holster. A little tag dangled from
the muzzle. "I forgot to get *un*peace-bonded when I left the
university! And *that* produced a surge of adrenaline you wouldn't
believe. And the adrenaline and the training did it. I was just
watching, from inside my own body. Usually, in a fight, a
hand or a foot is the *last* thing you want to hit with. That's
what pistols are for. Or machine guns."

"Your jacket is torn," she said.

"Cut," he replied, slipping four fingers into the slit. "The
gevlar vest turned the knife thrust."

"I'll ask the landlady if I can sew it up on her machine,"
Judith said. "Will you have supper with us?"

"You're a better cook than Schmitt," Karff said gallantly,
"even when you're sending out for tempeh."

From: Operation Malusian Pioneer
Subject: Conquest of Malusia
To: General Francisco Bloyer
Date: Day 164

    I. We have completed a preliminary survey of Malusia
and the Malusian Confederation.

    II. It is our considered opinion that there can be, and
will be, no resistance to an Imperial *coup de main*.

        A. Materially, Malusia is a basket case."

        B. Morally, Malusia is even worse.

    III. It is formally requested that these findings be pre-
sented to HIH the Regent.

      /s/

Senior Colonel S. T. Karff
    cc: Office of the Regent (Attn: Ct. Franz-Otto)

On the ISS *Grand Duke Grossnickel*, Lieutenant Colonel
Schrader set the memo on the polished expanse of General
Bloyer's desk. "The shit, sir, has hit the fan. Why in *hell* didn't
you push to get the operation moved to the base of the space
elevator?"

"Eeh," Bloyer replied, picking up the memo, "are you still
nagging about that?"

"No, sir. That's water over the dam, sir."

"Yes. I see that Karff is being his usual obnoxious self. Well, file it and forget it."

"Yes, sir. You think that no one in the Office of the Regent will read the information copy?"

"They got an information copy?" Bloyer snatched the memo. "Yes! Oh *damn!*" He stood up and began walking around the office with an agitated strut. "The son of a bitch. The son of a bitch! The son of a *bitch!*"

"Yes, sir," Schrader said. "File it and forget it. Right?"

"Nooo!"

"Very good, sir. How *do* you wish to handle the matter?"

"I don't know! The son of a bitch! Schrader, what am I going to do?"

"I would suggest that you arrange for his presentation, sir."

"The Grand Duke Sergius doesn't *want* to conquer Malusia."

"Yes, sir. You hope to curry favor by withholding information from him? You wish to spare him the pain of making a difficult decision? You seek to show him only those facts that he would want to see?"

"Don't get snotty, Schrader. Mainly I don't want Karff back."

"Yes, sir. In that case, I would suggest that you leave Operation Malusian Pioneer in place and bring Colonel Karff back by himself for his presentation. In one of the gliders."

"What good will that do?"

"You buy time, sir. When he finishes his report, say, 'This is very good. This is brilliant. But what about the space elevator? What about the cities at the base of the space elevator? Let's investigate them, also.' And send him back. You will, of course, have to move the transporter."

"I don't like it," Bloyer said.

"Yes, sir. Your alternative is to return Karff with the transporter. That might not be so bad if the Grand Duke really *doesn't* want to conquer Malusia. Of course Karff would be back."

"I don't like *that* either," Bloyer said.

"File it and forget it, sir?"

"No."

"What do you *suggest*, sir?"

* * *

The glider nestled in the cargo bay, its wings folded downward at the fuselage and extending beyond the cargo bay doors. Powered reels of gevlar filaments supported it at three points. Detana was in the cockpit checking out the life support systems. Under his windbreaker, Karff wore an emergency pressure vest, a good luck gesture intended to ward off catastrophe. The emergency pressure vest face mask hung at his throat; a sudden drop in pressure would push it on his face. He leaned against the railing on the cargo bay deck, watching Detana in the glider below.

"It's a thirty-six-hour trip," Judith said. "Do you have everything?" He nodded absently. "Your presentation?"

"It's on board," Karff said. "On top of my bag."

"Do you have a clean shirt?"

"Sure," he said, putting his arm around her shoulders. "You packed for me, remember?"

"Yes." Judith put her arm around his waist. "I just didn't want to forget anything."

Marika came up with a plastic bag. "Schmitt made some sandwiches," she said, "and I put in some oranges and boiled eggs. We have some tempeh, too. Would you like tempeh?" Tempeh was a soybean cake enriched with mycoprotein grown *in situ*, a delicately flavored fungoid confection, usually cooked in hot oil.

"Thank you, no," Karff said. "I don't like it cold." Hot, perhaps I could *learn* to like it, he thought. Still, any civilization that stopped the growing of tobacco because it was unhealthy *would* replace pizza with tempeh.

Outside, Aqua Pura was rising. Soon the Imperial Fleet would cross the terminator into the line of sight, and the window would open for his trip 'home.'

Detana climbed from the cockpit. "You're all set, Colonel. Good luck." He saluted, and Karff, holding a bag of sandwiches in one hand and Judith in the other, looked at him for a second.

"I'm not in uniform," Karff said at last. He let go of Judith and shook hands with his aide. "Thanks." He looked at his watch. The window was about to open. He kissed Judith and started to shake hands with Marika when she put her arms around him and gave him a hug.

"Good luck, big boy," she said in passable Imperiales.

78

"Thank you. Remember, when Judith tells you to keep it on, you keep it on."

Then he climbed into the glider, slid the canopy shut and sealed it, and started the reels of monofilament unwinding. Once the glider was clear of the cargo bay, the wings extended themselves and locked in place. Karff hit the release, and the glider hung beneath the cargo bay for a few seconds before it started to lose altitude. Then the FAD-200 caught it, and it rolled to one side and began to climb into the cool night air, making lazy circles as it rose above the transporter, climbing, climbing. Several hundred meters above, the tractor beam from the fleet picked it up, and the glider started to climb toward the shining crescent of Aqua Pura like a homesick angel.

Chapter 9.

Presentation to the Grand Duke

"YOU CAN'T WEAR that to the Red Audience Chamber," Count Franz-Otto said stiffly. "Where are your dress blacks?"

Karff pushed the yachting cap back on his head and smiled. "My *regular* blacks are in the suitcase. I *will* have time to change, won't I?"

"You should wear your *dress* blacks," the Count said.

"*What* dress blacks, Bunky? You talk like we left Portales on a bloody cruise liner!"

"Ah, yes..." Franz-Otto bit his lip. "You have about half an hour. Shave. Go to the bathroom. Don't change. If you can't wear dress blacks, go in costume. A minor impropriety would be shocking. Something as gross as what you're wearing *might* amuse His Imperial Highness." Karff felt his beard and nodded.

"Thanks a lot, Count."

The Red Audience Chamber was standing room only. Who was in good odor could generally be told by the seating arrangement.

"Quite a crowd," Karff murmured softly, looking out from the wings.

"Yes," Franz-Otto agreed. "Address them as 'Ladies and Gentlemen, My Lords, Honorable Regent'... are you *sure* you want to wear that windbreaker bright-side out?"

Karff shrugged. "If I'm going to be in costume..."

General Bloyer finished his introduction and Karff walked on stage. There was an audible gasp from the audience and a ripple of tittering. Karff flushed slightly and scowled.

"May it please the Regent," he said, "I bring back a spy's report on Malusia, and I stand before you in the garb of a Malusian fighter." He removed his windbreaker and displayed the device on the back. "Some of you will recognize the emblem, I am sure. The skull and crossbones of security, surrounded by the oak leaves of a colonel. The lettering, which you may *not* be able to read, says 'Imperial Union Goons.' It may interest you to know that the Malusian word for 'union goons' is *gestapo*. A rose, by any other name..." he smiled. "May we have the first slide, please?"

The first slide was a schematic diagram of the space elevator.

"Enkomi," Karff said, "is a diode. It permits the passage of commodities and people in one direction only. Down. Enkomi controls the operation of the space elevator, and it is defended at both ends. The Kaloutsa Naval Base, here, and the various military units stationed by Ayios Sostis, *here*. Since Enkomi is inaccessible except by elevator, there is no need to defend it, and it is not defended. Enkomi is *also* the banking center of the Malusian Confederation, in part because it is simultaneously central and inaccessible.

"It is the key to the conquest of Malusia, and it sits there for our taking.

"Let me review a little Malusian history so that you can better understand why this is so. The first habitats in this system were built by Mamnu colonists profoundly vexed with government. Not only their government, but all government. This is not a new situation by any means. What was different here was that a planet, Malusia, was being terraformed, modified to be suitable for human habitation.

"The problem the colonists faced was that populations will increase unless held sternly in check. For a time they solved this problem by building new habitats. And then, at about the time the number of habitats was reaching the point where coalitions and protogovernments would start to form, were perhaps already forming, they made an astonishing move.

"They created the Malusian Confederation in order to build the space elevator. And when the space elevator was built, Malusia was opened to colonization. A remarkable thing. The Malusian Confederation was a successful compromise, just enough government to keep a real government from forming, and by opening Malusia it drained off the surplus population that might otherwise have gone into new and progovernment habitats. That was eight centuries ago.

"Originally, when commodities went down, an equivalent

81

mass of organic matter or fertilizer went up. As the population on the planet increased, the demand for commodities increased. The loads going down increased, and the loads going up dwindled into nothingness. The next slide, please."

The next slide showed the gross tonnage moved on the space elevator for the previous three hundred years. Blue going into space, red going to the planet. The blue line started near the bottom and stayed there. The red line rose toward a dotted line marked "design limit," and fell back from it in a sawtooth curve, three times in 163 years. Each time, it fell back less far, and each time it rose higher before falling.

"We are *here*," Karff said. "Substantially above the design limit of the space elevator. The sawtooth curve represents a drop in shipments caused by the disruption of service in the space elevator. In each case, the disruption was accompanied by widespread famine, which reduced the demand for commodities to where the space elevator could cope with it.

"Why, you ask, doesn't the Malusian Confederation build a second space elevator? I was told that they can't afford it.

"That being the case, why doesn't the Malusian Confederation permit the inhabitants of Malusia to grow their own food? The answer is, If Malusia could feed itself it would form its own government! And *that* the Great Holders will not permit!

"What we are looking at, Ladies and Gentlemen, My Lords, Honorable Regent, is an established anarchy more than eight hundred years old. Quite possibly the oldest anarchic regime in human history. What will they do if a government forms itself on Malusia? What can they do? Destruction with nuclear weapons is a real possibility.

"What is this to us? We have problems of our own as I need hardly remind you. I submit that the choices facing the Great Holders are profoundly demoralizing. Faced with an Imperial conquest which would relieve them of the necessity of making either choice, I believe that they would be unable to resist. They would be *unable* to resist in any event, due to their archaic armament. What I meant was that they would not have the *will* to offer resistance.

"Malusia, in my judgment, lacks both the will and the means to resist. We can pick it like a ripe fruit—an overripe fruit. We have but to decide that we want it, we have only to reach out our hand for it, and it is ours!"

There was a ripple of polite applause. Clearly, the audience liked the idea but didn't want to commit itself until the Regent gave them an idea of whether he approved.

"What problems may we anticipate? First, a war is always destructive. We might have to feed Malusia after we take it. I believe it should be no problem, even in the worst case, which is the complete and permanent destruction of the supply lines. Malusiopolis sits in the middle of a continent-size peat bog hundreds of meters deep. Local industry already exists to convert peat into methane and methyl alcohol. Methyl alcohol is the feedstock for growing single-cell protein, and there exists an effectively unlimited supply.

"The second problem is that imposing a government, *our* government, might be difficult. Antigovernment attitudes are deeply ingrained. That, however, is a problem that can be solved at our leisure.

"The third problem is not a Malusian problem. If we take Enkomi, and the Rebel Fleet appears, what then? We won't be able to fight. Not now, nor a year from now. However, we *can* hide. We can go to ground around Malusiopolis, and when . . ."

"And when the Rebel Fleet says, 'Who's there?', you can say, 'Nobody but us chickens, boss!'" Bloyer shouted sarcastically.

"Perhaps," Karff said, gazing at his chief with lifted eyebrows. "I expect you've given the problem more thought than I have." Pressing on, he returned to the picture being displayed. "The next slide is a cutaway model of Enkomi. In the event that we *do* wish to take it, two routes appear both obvious and easy . . ."

When he finished, the audience was silent. Then the Regent stood up, applauding, and the Imperial Household followed suit, giving him a standing ovation.

Afterward, in the Robing Chamber, Karff found himself with the Grand Duke Sergius, Count Franz-Otto, and General Bloyer, only too aware that he was a small fish socializing with sharks. Franz-Otto served brandied coffee all around.

"A very interesting presentation, Colonel," Sergius commented. "Do you *really* think that we can pluck Malusia like overripe fruit?"

"Yes, sir. There is no mutual loyalty between ruler and

83

ruled, no emotional bond of any sort, only the cold rationality of mutual self-interest. And against an outside threat, the lower classes *must* feel that they have no stake, so why should they fight?"

"Interesting, if true." Sergius fingered his mustache. "But after so much time, there should be an emotional tie of some sort. How could there not be?"

Karff sipped his brandied coffee. "Because the Great Holders have been at pains to keep such a tie from forming. They feel that patriotism would push Malusia in the direction of a Malusian state—of a central government—and since they don't *need* patriotism, they don't stir it up."

"Possibly so. Yet if the Imperial Fleet were suddenly to appear, wouldn't that shock *develop* Malusian patriotism?"

"I don't know, sir," Karff replied. "Suppose it did? There are no institutions capable of channeling it against us."

"Ah . . . Karff," General Bloyer said, "you *must* have noticed the resemblance of the Malusian situation to the classical campaign at Lyonsk. And yet you recommend striking directly at Enkomi. Surely you are not ignorant of military history?"

"Malusia is not Lyonsk. And the situations are not similar. Only the general layout of the Malusian system around the space elevator is similar. There is a *great* difference in weaponry."

"There is some difference in weapons," Bloyer conceded, "but don't you agree that the best, the most *professional* manner of proceeding would be to seize one or two of the strongest habitats, and then, at our leisure take Malusiopolis, the city at the center of the Malusian landmass?"

"No, sir. Enkomi is the choke point. It is defended from the ground, and from the Kaloutsa Naval Base above, but I could take it with a couple of companies of marines. The defense doesn't believe that Enkomi is accessible except by space elevator, so only the elevator is defended. The other thing is that the so-called Malusian landmass is a stinking peat bog. There is no point whatsoever in going there."

"I fear you have been in operations too long, Colonel Karff," Bloyer said coldly. "Have you *been* to Enkomi?"

"No, sir. So far we haven't been able to schedule FAD time to transfer the transporter." *Your* department, you ass-licking wimp. "I *have* been to Malusiopolis."

"No doubt you are infatuated with your own brilliant conclusions, Colonel Karff. Nevertheless, the fact is that you have *not* been to Enkomi, the place you propose to seize with a tiny handful of marines."

"Yes, sir."

"And *you* haven't been to Malusia, General Bloyer," Sergius said. "The resemblance to Lyonsk may well be superficial. Why don't we send Colonel Karff and the transporter to the base of the space elevator? After he studies Enkomi at first hand, he may agree with you."

"Yes, sir," General Bloyer said. "*If* we can schedule FAD time."

"Count Franz-Otto will attend to that detail. Tell me, Colonel, is it really true that the ideological justification the Great Holders make for themselves is that they prevent a central government from forming?"

"Yes, sir. Even here, it is understood that anarchy is a very unstable form of government."

After Karff and Bloyer left, the Count eased the Regent's velvet smoking jacket off his shoulders and hung it on the pipe rack.

"What do you think?" Sergius asked.

"More scouting is probably a good idea, sir."

"No, no. I meant about their judgment." Franz-Otto took the Regent's dress tunic and slipped it on over his arms.

"I think they both show good judgment, sir. Karff is just looking at the smaller picture. We can *always* do it his way, can't we?"

Sergius studied himself in the full-length mirror for a moment as Franz-Otto fastened his tunic.

"Perhaps," he said at last. "Karff made one excellent point. If we seize Enkomi, we can go to ground around Malusiopolis—Moptown, he called it. Then, when the Rebel Fleet shows up..."

"As Bloyer put it, sir, 'There's nobody here but us chickens!'"

Sergius nodded. "A cheap shot, I think. Following *his* plan, the Rebels would find us all over the inner system. They couldn't miss us. Do you suppose he's trying to stall us?"

"What for, sir?"

"Just a thought, Count. A passing fancy. I'm paranoid, but

am I paranoid *enough*? Do you know anything more about either of those two?"

"Indirectly, sir."

Sergius admired himself in the mirror, stroking his mustache. "Yes?"

"Elise, my mistress, used to be with Karff. She came on board with some jewelry and gave it to him for safekeeping. The refugees were sleeping in a barracks at that point, and she was afraid it would be stolen. One of Bloyer's henchmen forced her to spy on Karff, and he caught her at it. As she put it, he invited her to leave, but he returned the jewelry. Bloyer's henchmen—"

"Subordinate," Sergius said gently.

"Bloyer's subordinate insisted that *he* be given the jewelry for safekeeping, and he wound up keeping some of the best pieces. On the record, Bloyer chose Colonel Himmelreich over Senior Colonel Karff to run the mother transporter."

"Himmelreich was the henchman in question?"

"Yes, sir."

"So Bloyer tolerates a little larceny on his staff," Sergius mused. "Larceny and stupidity, just as long as they are loyal. Karff," he said, putting on his white gloves, "may be an honorable man, but he is *not* a team player."

Chapter 10.
Revision of Pattern for Conquest, I

IN THE LIGHT of the evening sun, Ayios Sostis shone like burnished gold, a gleaming coin on the brazen ocean. At night it would become a garland of multicolored lights, never lovelier than when seen from above and at a great distance, but now the flat canopy of glass that covered the city caught the light of the sun and transmuted it to pure gold.

Seen closer, the canopy was not flat, but a gently sloping cone that rose abruptly into a slender spire more than two thousand meters tall. From the tip of that spire was appended a jaunty white plume, a billowing white cumulus cloud that began forming shortly after sunrise, and that extended for hundreds of kilometers by evening. Visible from space, it was a reference point for navigation in all but the worst of storms.

The spire, which was actually quite robust if not scandalously overbuilt, enclosed a cluster of huge pipes, each one enclosing a windmill of multimegawatt capacity. The canopy served as the solar collector to drive those windmills. The morning sun, shining through the glass, warmed the air beneath, causing it to rise, and as it rose, the warm air must necessarily move closer to the center, as cool air entered at the periphery to replace it. The internal geometry of Ayios Sostis imparted a spin, and the warm and humid air entered the pipes of the spire with considerable energy. Some of that energy was used to drive the turbines. Finally, when the spent air, saturated with water vapor, was vented into the cool air above, it relaxed from its arduous labors and formed a cloud.

Underneath the canopy, Ayios Sostis was a city of blocks, each block composed of three or four or six hexagonal prisms, each prism slip cast from reinforced concrete and bonded to its block with bands of stainless steel. Three cables anchored each prism to the seamount, 6,730 meters below, and maintained in constant tension. The westerly equatorial current displaced the city sixty to seventy meters west of the anchoring site. At low tide more nearly seventy meters, at high tide more nearly sixty.

The space elevator, in contrast to the power spire, was off-center and inconspicuous, a black hairline marked by winking red warning lights. It was mounted over the main ship channel, and allowed all the room to move, relative to the city, that it could need. Covering the long slot in the canopy was a collar attached to the space elevator, which rested on an air cushion which rested on the canopy. The canopy and the space elevator slid freely back and forth without losing any of the entrapped air that drove the windmills.

"Very strange," Detana commented at last.

Karff looked up. "What did you see, Captain?"

"The space elevator. It's running in the down-only mode almost all the time. They must have power to burn. Why is Ayios Sostis using *wind* power?"

"The Great Holders make more money selling spare parts for the turbines and generators than they would selling cheap electricity," Karff replied.

"Right," Detana said. "But the cheap electricity . . . what do the Great Holders *do* with it?"

Ildenhagen looked up from the controls. "There's a plume of warmish water due west of Ayios Sostis. Check out the infrared pictures we took on the way down. None of the other cities had one, only Ayios Sostis. Ten to one they use the current generated by the space elevator to heat the ocean."

"What a waste," Detana said.

"Absolutely," Karff agreed. "Of course, why should anarchists run things any better than anyone else?"

"What are anarchists doing with central banks?" Detana asked. "Are you sure they aren't libertarians?"

"Hah!" said Ildenhagen. "Anarchists have to put their money *somewhere*. If they have money, how could they not have banks?"

"Right on," Karff said. "After a time any -archy will settle down. Anarchy is usually so unstable it never gets the chance, but states always have the same problems, and the solution to those problems—once you refine the design a little—always looks pretty much the same. Besides, anarchists and libertarians—what's the difference?"

"Libertarians are anarchists on the gold standard," Ildenhagen said.

"Hey," Detana protested, "there's a *lot* of difference!"

"Sure there is," Karff said as he poured himself a cup of coffee from the thermos. "Doctrinal disputes between religious heresies are the most intractable differences you'll ever find. But an outsider can't tell them apart. Except for their religion, all those Churches are alike. Now speaking as a pillar of the capital-S State, *I* don't see any difference."

Detana shrugged. "I think we may be dealing with libertarians, not anarchists. That's all."

"After eight hundred years in power," Karff said, "you are dealing with the immensely rich Great Holders. They own everything, and what they are—what they have *got* to be—is conservative as hell. Are they anarchists or libertarians?"

"They have a gold-based currency," Detana said. "Libertarian?"

"No," Karff said. "After eight hundred years in power what they are is rich. Their rhetoric *explains* it, their theology *justifies* it. And they'll kill to keep it." He took a sip of coffee. "The topopolitical configuration in this system is bizarre. There are thirteen habitats altogether, feeding a planet that has never been permitted to become even remotely self-sustaining. Why? What do the Great Holders get out of it?"

"Money?" Ildenhagen suggested.

"No . . ." Karff shook his head. "Locally, they seem wedded to the idea that money is gold and vice versa. And all the gold there is, the Great Holders mine and refine out in space. What do you think, Detana?"

"Not service. Any service they need they can get out in the habitats easier and cheaper. What?"

Karff sipped his coffee and watched the sunset through the Bridge windows. "A sink," he said at last. "A population sink. The Malusian Confederation drains its excess population off into Malusia. And feeds them. And every couple of generations thins them out with a famine. And the space elevator keeps the poor bastards in their place!"

"That reminds me," Ildenhagen said, "Judith says you can't

book passage up on the space elevator. Not with the travel agents, not with anybody."

"That figures." Karff looked thoughtful. "I expect you need an invitation to get back into space. That explains why they never picked up on mechanically simulated telekinesis, though. Knowledge diffuses, and *that* knowledge would have destabilized the whole system."

"I don't follow you, Colonel."

"The space elevator is what keeps the surplus population from going to where the food is. The *failure* of the space elevator is what justifies the famines that keeps the population level. If FADs were available, the whole house of cards would come tumbling down. A good thing, too, I'd say."

"Hey," Ildenhagen said, "they don't have revolutions."

"Right," Detana added. "They don't have wars, either."

"Not having wars is unnatural," Karff said. "Besides, there are worse things than dying in a war."

"Like what?"

"Like living on Malusia," Karff said. "You're on the bottom *forever!*"

Thorikos lay forty-one kilometers northwest of Ayios Sostis, if measured from edge to edge. Measured center to center, it was sixty-one kilometers. From the western edge of Thorikos, extending beyond its glass canopy, was the municipal airport and the barracks of the Delian 3rd Marine Division. The radars, missiles, and aircraft hangars of the Delians occupied a block of six hexagonal prisms at the eastern end of the runway. The runways, terminal, and airport control tower floated on concrete pontoons anchored at the eastern end only. A propellor-driven flying wing marked "Air Corsikos" had touched down and was taxiing toward the terminal.

There had been several reasons for landing at the airport, and in the daytime. While it might have been possible to fly the transporter under the glass canopy over Ayios Sostis, it seemed highly impractical, and not terribly inconspicuous. Cutting or otherwise breaking through a canopy which had no holes in it also seemed to be undesirable. By way of contrast, the airport was open, accessible, and a natural entryway. Which closed at night.

"Air Corsikos three thirty-seven is the last scheduled flight today," Detana said, from the radar room.

Karff nodded and stepped inside. "Wish me luck," he said. They shook hands and he walked back to the cargo bay deck. Schmitt, the lawyer who did the cooking, slung his bag over his shoulder and tightened the straps. Judith handed him a string of firecrackers with a pull-wire igniter.

"Do you think Marika will be all right back at the apartment?" she asked.

"Sure," Karff said. "Didn't you tell me she knocked them dead down at the Club Enkomi without taking off *anything*?"

"So I did," Judith said. "Are *you* all right?"

"I couldn't spit to save my life," Karff said, tucking his cap inside the windbreaker.

Stavo's voice came over the intercom. "Your attention, please," he said. "The FAD is set. Repeat, the FAD is set."

A spot of red light appeared on the other side of the guard rail.

"Good luck, Colonel," Schmitt called.

Judith waved but said nothing.

Karff tossed them a salute in acknowledgment and stepped over the rail. He hesitated for a moment. Then he let go and dropped through the cargo bay doors.

"Good luck, Thibalt!" Judith called.

The FAD lowered him into the afternoon air, swinging him laterally and down until he was over the main stairway leading to the water taxis.

At thirty meters he pulled the ignition-wire on the firecrackers and threw them. The pedestrians below scattered or dropped flat. Stavo landed him a few meters from the edge of the stairway and Karff stepped over a woman and ran down the stairs. At the first landing he stopped and put on his cap. While he was unslinging the bag for easier carrying, the woman came down the stairs.

"What was *that*?" he asked.

"Some idiot lit a string of firecrackers," she said. "I saw the last of them going off."

On the dock he looked around until he saw the limousine serving the Ayios Sostis Ferry, a gaudily painted hydrofoil with enclosed seats.

An hour later he walked into the Hotel Atheniou.

The Atheniou was famed for its superlative kitchen, its posh accommodations, and the excellence of its service. In the lobby, potted palms flanked a bronze statue of Hercules holding aloft an astrolabe as he stood on a great bronze turtle. The turtle, in turn, rested on the curved back of still another turtle, submerged in a pool of dark water, which poured off one end in a waterfall and was returned at the other in a voluminous fountain. After a moment a holographic face appeared in the waterfall and said, "It's turtles all the way down."

Karff smiled and walked over to the registration desk. The desk clerk studiously ignored him. After ninety seconds Karff took out a fifty-dolar gold piece and spun it on the counter. Nothing. The rattle of the coin unwinding on the countertop didn't affect the clerk in the slightest. Karff spun it again. Nothing. The third time he spun it, he sent it spinning on to the other side of the counter. The clerk gave up. He didn't want some backwoods hick jumping the counter, so he walked over and handed the coin back to Karff without a word.

"Thank you, young fella," Karff said. "I don't suppose you'd have a room for tonight, would you?"

"No, mister. We're full up."

"Pity," Karff said. "I'll have to take a suite, then, won't I?"

"The Delian Suite is available," the clerk said, somewhat taken aback. "That would be twelve hundred and fifty dolars a night. Payable in advance."

"I'll be staying a few days." Karff reached into his jacket pocket and drew out a stack of fifty 100-dolar bills. "Put me down for four nights."

"Yes, sir," the clerk said, counting the money. "Will there be anything else, sir?"

"I'll take supper in my room. After supper I want to see some business suits. I'm one-oh-six long, and I'd have them tailored, but there isn't time."

"The Barney Sessile Haberdasher's is across the street, sir. I'll have them send up a man for you after supper. Front!"

Barney Sessile himself came up with an assistant to move the rack of suits. After Karff had made his selections and the selections had been marked for alterations, Mr. Sessile bowed and smiled. "A most excellent choice, sir. May I suggest gold buttons with your own device or crest? A very distinctive accessory, and only six hundred dolars for three sets." Karff picked up his windbreaker and displayed the insignia of the Imperial Gestapo.

"Can you work from this?"

"Of course, sir," Mr. Sessile said. "May I suggest that the inscription be omitted? 'Imperial Union Goons' can hardly ingratiate you with any of the Great Holders."

"A good point." Karff nodded. "How do you make the buttons?"

"We have a computer," Sessile's assistant said. "We put the drawing on the platen, and the computer projects two views into a stereoscopic viewer. We can adjust it until it looks properly three dimensional. Then the computer uses a laser to make a series of cross-sectional cuts on a ribbon of steel. We stack them and bolt them together, and that's the male and female die. You can have the buttons stamped from ten-karat gold sheet for only a little extra."

"The gold-clad brass will be fine," Karff said. "They *will* be ready in the morning?"

"Oh, yes, sir," Mr. Sessile said. "I guarantee it."

"Fine. I'll pay half now, and half on delivery."

After the suits were delivered the next morning, Karff called for room service. A bellhop appeared at the door with impressive promptness, and Karff handed him a note written on hotel stationery.

"Please deliver this to Madame Sardikos," he said. He did *not* add, "—in the Naxian Suite, just down the hall." It would have been inappropriate to display such knowledge. A short time later his phone rang.

"Mr. Thibalt?" a woman's voice said.

"Speaking," Karff said, and then, less brusquely, "that is, I am he."

"You have a letter of introduction to the Madame?"

"From her nephew, Professor Jules Pargos-Sardikos. Yes. May I present myself?" There was a pause.

"Please do so. The Madame inquires if you would join us for lunch, say, at eleven-thirty?"

"I should be delighted. Where?"

"In the Naxian Suite. Turn right from your door and take the first left."

The first left took him to a pair of glass doors manned by Sardikan security officers. When he told them he had an engagement for lunch with Madame Sardikos, they let him in, passing him through the metal detector. There was a buzz.

"You seem to be carrying a bit of metal, sir," the senior officer said.

"I often do." Karff removed a handful of gold coins from his pants pocket. This time the detector was silent.

"Very good, sir. The next door." Karff checked his watch: 11:34. He was discreetly late, so that he would not appear eager, and sufficiently punctual so that lunch would not be inconvenienced. He checked himself in the gilt-framed pier glass set between the windows on the opposite wall. An immaculate suit of nubby white silk, white kid shoes, white silk tie, a charcoal brown shirt, handkerchief and skullcap, and personalized if slightly sinister gold buttons. Very impressive, he decided, and knocked on the door.

A woman answered. "Are you Mr. Thibalt?" she asked.

"Yes. I had the pleasure of chatting with you earlier today, I believe. You are—"

"I am Miss Melina, the Madame's secretary. Please follow me." The Naxian Suite was a duplicate of the Delian Suite. The same lofty ceilings, the same chandeliers, the same gold and white treatment of the woodwork. The furniture was different. Perhaps a concession to Madame Sardikos.

Herself was an elegantly lean woman in gauzy black silk, with beautifully coiffed white hair and a commanding presence. She might have been sixty or more; it was hard to tell. Money does that to people, Karff thought, especially when they've always had it. Anything that can be done, money can get done for you. He walked over to her, carrying himself with the grace of the Imperial Court. When she extended her hand, he bowed and kissed it. Then he handed her his letter of introduction.

"Sit down while I read what my idiot nephew has to say about you, Mr. Thibalt," she said. He perched in an ornate and uncomfortable chair while she put on her glasses and read the letter. "So. You impressed Jules, somewhat. How did you meet him?"

"Through a mutual acquaintance," Karff said. "A dissipated and vulgar journalist who holds him in high regard."

"A pity Jules does not seek the approbation of a better class of people. What do *you* think of my nephew, Mr. Thibalt?"

"What can I tell you?" Karff shook his head. "Jules is totally incompetent, but he'd provide the theoretical justification for the worst sort of thuggery if he thought it was 'underraising a government.' I think it's a mistake to keep him in Malusiopolis."

94

"He doesn't like it," she said, watching Karff closely. "You don't urge me to bring my own dear nephew back into the light of civilized society?"

"I have my own agenda. I don't even urge you to pay his allowance on time."

"Ah." She smiled. "For once, Jules surprises me. After lunch you can tell me about this agenda of yours."

Lunch was a clear soup and shrimp cocktail with sherbet for dessert. After Miss Melina cleared the dishes away, Madame Sardikos sat back in her green velvet easy chair and fingered her pearl necklace.

"You are a remarkably ignorant man to be so cultured," she said at last. "You mentioned a private agenda; what is it?"

"Better to have said 'remarkably cultured to be so ignorant.'" Karff reached into his jacket pocket. "In either case, I take it as a compliment." He took out a little plastic bag filled with a light tan powder and handed it to her.

"That is single-cell protein, SCP for short. It has two virtues. First, it can be produced in quantities limited only by the availability of one's feedstock, usually methyl alcohol. Second, it is a complete food. You might not want to live on it exclusively, but you could. Unfortunately, it is a bland, boring, monotonous main course.

"In my room I have plans for a pilot plant producing nine and a half tons a day. I didn't draw them up, and I didn't invent the process, and there is really no point in explaining how I came by them. However, it seems to me that the Great Holders must be interested . . ." He smiled. "Forgive me. I should not have said 'must' to a Great Holder in her own house. Nonetheless . . ."

Madame Sardikos held the bag in her hand and studied it for a few seconds.

"What a little thing it is," she said, putting it beside her coffee cup. "Well, Mr. Thibalt, *I* am interested. Now tell me, Why should the other Great Holders be interested?"

"It is hardly a secret that the space elevator which feeds Malusia is running above its rated capacity." Karff sat back on an ornately carved and lacquered loveseat in a futile attempt to get comfortable. "Jules tells me the Great Holders can't afford to build another one. This process would reduce the load the space elevator would have to carry. The alternative is to continue until the elevator breaks down, and suffer famine until the elevator is repaired." He crossed his legs. "Widespread famine."

"The famine would not be widespread, if, indeed, there were a famine at all," Madame Sardikos replied coldly. "Ample food has been stockpiled in Ayios Sostis to carry us through any time of temporary shortage. Indeed, everyone whom the Great Holders have an obligation to feed *will* be fed."

Karff uncrossed his legs and leaned forward. "And the food stocks in Moptown," he said gently. "What of them?"

"Don't be impertinent, young man! And don't say 'Moptown.' Malusiopolis is a perfectly adequate name."

"Yes, Madame." Karff refilled his coffee cup. "Malusiopolis has about ten days' supply of wheat, five days of dried potatoes, thirteen of soybeans. A little rice, a little barley. How long will the elevator be out of service?"

Madame Sardikos fingered her pearls and said nothing.

"The average for the last three outages was a hundred and eight days," he said. "The last outage was for a hundred twenty-one. Who must be fed in Malusiopolis?"

"No one."

"Not even Jules?"

"Not even Jules."

Karff took a sip of coffee. "Well," he said at last. "I realize that the Great Holders are reluctant to give Malusia any measure of independence lest those evil people should conspire together to form a government. But if, God forbid, they *should* form a government, what would you do, you Great Holders?"

"You should not talk to the Madame so!" Miss Melina protested.

"It is all right, Melina. He knows, and I know he knows, that we would destroy them. Although I must confess that the prospect appalls some of us."

"That speaks well of your humanity," Karff said gently. "I realize that this must be decided in a collegial manner among all the Great Holders, so I would like to go to Enkomi to talk with them."

"For one so ignorant, you have a remarkable instinct for the jugular. I can take you to Enkomi, but I may not be able to bring you back. Are you sure you want to go?"

He shifted his weight. "The issue is too important not to go."

"What issue?"

"Ideology," Karff said softly. "When your ideology forces you to choose between starving your own people and killing them if they try to feed themselves, you ought to think about finding another ideology." He picked up the little bag of tan powder. "You can no longer starve us at your pleasure, Madame. You must choose between your ideology and mass murder."

The next morning Miss Melina informed him that a special car had been arranged to take them up the space elevator to Enkomi, and that he must be ready to leave no later than 11:00 AM.

Karff packed his bag and contemplated his fine new clothes spread out on the bed. Finally he called Barney Sessile and told them to bring over a suitcase to pack them in. The bellhop arrived with a beautiful top-of-the-line piece of luggage while he was having a leisurely breakfast.

Shortly before the appointed moment of departure, Miss Melina, looking harassed and bothered, demanded to know if he was ready to leave. Karff put his yachting cap over the navy skullcap and slipped on his windbreaker, dark-side out, while his two bags were carefully stacked on the third of three baggage carts.

In the hall a number of security officers and hotel people milled around, and finally the baggage carts took the freight elevator down to the docking level on the first trip, while Madame Sardikos, Miss Melina, and Karff, with the security officers, took it down on the second trip.

When they reached their level, the baggage was already being loaded, carts and all, on one of the hotel's courtesy yachts. Karff walked out to the end of the pier and looked around.

The view was uninspiring. Windowless gray concrete walls made 120° angles with each other. A lattice work of unpainted metal girders kept the hexagonal prisms in their place. Stainless steel, probably, softened by the patina of age. A foot bridge, swinging gently in the wind. Trash floating on the dark water. A faint, foul odor. And overall, the glass canopy that tempered the blue of the Malusian sky to a hazy glare.

This place is too orderly, he decided. There ought to be seagulls. Seagulls and graffiti. Maybe even advertising.

Aboard the yacht he stood near the bow, ignoring the

security man standing at his elbow, and watched as it made its way toward the ship channel, the terminus of the space elevator.

A cargo vessel bearing the crest of Delos was being loaded with containers of some sort, perhaps wheat. Two others waited in line.

Below the terminus, Karff saw that although the elevator ended, the cable did not. This end, the merest thread compared to the other, was a black, shining pillar, perhaps a meter thick, that was anchored in the bedrock of the seamount thousands of meters below. Above, elevator and cable passed through a tiny chink of blue in the canopy that permitted the space elevator to sway back and forth.

Actually, he thought, it is the city that moves, swayed by wind and tide. The space elevator is far more massive than the city, and far stronger.

The courtesy yacht docked, and they waited on a long pier while their baggage was loaded. When they saw the empty carts returning, the security men escorted the party to the boarding elevator, which took them through the glass canopy to an open platform where their car waited for them to board. Karff looked out over Ayios Sostis. The cluster of pipes generating power from the ever-blowing wind was impressive. Otherwise, he was looking through a glass darkly at a sullen and docile city he didn't understand.

Two of the security men boarded the space elevator with them, and Miss Melina served lunch from a hamper the hotel had packed. The trip to Enkomi took two hours and ten minutes.

Karff addressed the Enkomi Chamber of Commerce in a long room paneled with cherry wood and floored with white oak parquet. From the mirrored ceiling hung three ornate and tasteless chandeliers whose flash and glitter were reflected and rereflected from the great gilt-frame mirrors at each end of the room.

His audience comprised twenty men and eight women, Great Holders without exception. As he had watched them arriving in their white suits and black dresses, he had remarked to Miss Melina that they looked very ordinary. "When you are where *they* are," she said, "whom do you want to impress?" They sat at round tables draped with beige linen, and before each of them was set a neatly printed name plate, listing name and holding. They looked old, as if they had been carved from weathered wood, the Great Holders, and impassive.

"That concludes the technical details," Karff said as he leaned on the podium. "Your own laboratories are in the process of confirming them with the samples they were given.

"When you have independently confirmed these data, the next step is to build a pilot plant. For this, a line of credit of not more than ten million dolars would——"

"This has to be against our interest, sir," a silvery-haired man with dark eyebrows and dark eyes said. Mr. John Naxos-Limnion of Naxos. "If Malusia is able to feed itself, how can it be prevented from forming a government?" There were murmurs of "Hear, hear," and "No government."

"The Great Holders have systematically prevented the Malusians from feeding themselves," Karff agreed. "Dr. Naxos-Limnion stands firmly in accord with historical tradition on that point. There is, however, another historical tradition. In the past one hundred sixty-three years there have been no less than three failures of the space elevator, the most recent forty-two years ago in 783. The '83, they call it in Malusiopolis. In each case there was widespread famine."

"There was no famine in '83," Dr. Naxos-Limnion replied with some vigor. "I deny it, sir, and I was there."

"In Malusiopolis? You didn't feed people who couldn't feed themselves for more than six months. How could there *not* be a famine?"

"Ample supplies of food were stored on Malusia in '83," said Madilene Cretos, from Cretos, a rather plump woman with hennaed hair. "Ample supplies are stored there today."

"Malusia is a planet, Madame," Karff said gently, "and distribution is also a problem. There were ample supplies in Ayios Sostis in the '83, but Thorikos lost one in twenty, Milatos and Karysto lost one in ten, and Malusiopolis lost one in five."

"You can't prove that," she said, "you have no proof."

Karff reached into his pocket and took out a blue-covered pamphlet.

"This is a scurrilous diatribe and polemic entitled *Malusiopolis: Asshole of the Universe*," he said. "Nevertheless, the author has compiled figures, and I have checked some of them, and the '83 is undoubted historical fact. I have another copy if you'd like to read it."

"No." Madame Cretos shook her head. "No, thank you."

"The '83 is history," Karff continued. "Not ancient history; Dr. Naxos-Limnion was there, after all, and the rest of you were living at the time, though not, perhaps, in positions of authority. It is now 825, and the space elevator is again verging on a breakdown." Perhaps, he thought, during the winter vacation at the university so that your grandchildren can return to safety. Best not to say it—the argument will be emotional enough as it is.

"*Malusia* does not face a famine. Malusia, after all is a planet. But the Malusian people will endure great suffering. *They* face a famine and an unnecessary famine—it need not happen.

"In fact, Ladies and Gentlemen, it is not going to happen! The technology I have just shown you is already dispersed. You may authorize its use, or it will be used anyway, but one way or another it will be used!"

"No, by God!" said a burly, bald-headed man, Gregor Naxos of Naxos. "You plant the seed of government, and I will have no government!"

"No government!" echoed around the room.

"You wish to impose a famine on your own people?" Karff asked. "Surely you do not!"

"I will have no government!" Naxos repeated.

"Very good. I assure you that no government is intended. I am sure that no famine is intended either, but the space elevator is presently operating at one hundred and nine percent of capacity—"

"One hundred and nineteen percent," a woman said.

"—One hundred and nineteen percent of capacity, and a failure of the space elevator appears probable in the near future. At which time, famine will occur whether you want one or not. Certainly no provision has been made to prevent it."

"But I , Gregor Naxos, tell you that there will be no famine!"

"Gregor is right," said John Melian-Melosian of Melos, an old man with gnarled hands. "It is axiomatic that if a people can feed themselves, they will form a government to make sure they all eat the same. In time, and every time, they will form a government."

"No government! No government!" the cry was repeated several times, but not by everyone, and not by the women.

"So keep the space elevator running, or build another one," Karff said. "That way the problem never arises."

There was a long silence. "We can't," a woman conceded at last.

"I am not talking about forming a government," Karff said. "I am talking about feeding the hungry. I am talking about feeding the cities of Malusia when the space elevator stops."

"I think we ought to do it," Madame Sardikos said, playing with her string of pearls. "Gregor can't wish away the impending failure of the space elevator, and I for one, find the consequences too terrible to ignore."

"I disagree," Dr. Naxos-Limnion said. "It is by no means certain that the space elevator will fail, and if a few groundlings starve, why, so what?"

"They are *our* people," said Madame Sardikos. "And when was the last time *you* missed a meal, Johnny?"

"They bred without permission," said a lean, leathery man with a thin mustache. "If they die, what of it?"

"Excuse me," Karff said. "Bred without *whose* permission?"

"Mine," General Delosian said. "Ours, actually. Malusia belongs to all our family—we are one family here, no matter what some of us say—and our people will do as we tell them!"

"Damn straight!" Naxos yelled. "And if they don't, they get the boot! Screw up, it's the Kalavassos, sonny boy! Or exile. And no way home!"

Karff pulled his nose between thumb and forefinger. "It appears that my principals have failed to anticipate your wishes. Nevertheless, when the space elevator breaks down, as I assure you it will, and when Malusiopolis then starts to feed itself, as I assure you it will, what are you going to do about it?"

"Nuke them," General Delosian spat.

That ended the discussion. In the argument that followed, Delosian received qualified support from Gregor Naxos and Dr. Naxos-Limnion alone.

On the question of producing single-cell protein, Madame Sardikos, Madame Cretos, and a Dr. Natan Sardikos supported Karff, ten were against him, and fifteen were undecided. The matter was tabled for future consideration.

Chapter 11.
The Penetration of Enkomi

AFTER THE MEETING, the Great Holders began to caucus on the question. The Naxos group in the Taverna Sounion, three levels up, the Sardikos group in the Vasilia Cafe, down the hall a few hundred meters.

"There hasn't been a dust-up like this since I can remember," Madame Sardikos said with grim satisfaction. "Miss Melina, I want you to stay with Mr. Thibalt and see that he doesn't get turned around. You hear?"

Miss Melina, a very tailored woman with hair of indeterminate color drawn up into a tight bun, blinked her pale blue eyes.

"What does the Madame mean?"

"What I said. Stay with him. There may be an attempt to buy him off if it looks like we have a chance to get the votes."

"But Madame ... Mr. Thibalt is an able speaker. Couldn't he help you in the caucus?"

"He doesn't know the people." Madame Sardikos fingered her rope of pearls. "Besides, he isn't a team player. I couldn't rely on him to do what I wanted. This is Great Holder business, and, of course, he isn't one of us."

"But Madame ..." Miss Melina looked distressed. "What if he makes advances?"

"We'll have a surgeon put your maidenhead back in place. Don't worry about it. And don't lose him!"

"Yes, Madame."

Melina found Karff with three Great Holders, two men and a woman, in the hotel bar across the hall from the conference room.

"'... so *then* that pig sounded the alarm, rescued the baby and saved the farmhouse from burning down!' 'Yes, yes,' said the salesman, 'but the pegleg, what happened to his leg?' Well, the farmer pushed his straw hat back on his head. 'Mister,' he said, 'a pig like *that* you don't eat all at once!'"

The tall man smiled politely. The short man looked as if he were waiting for the punch line. The woman put down her drink.

"Well, of course—" she said.

Karff turned to Melina. "Hello, darling—do you know George and John-Peter Skyros and Madame Lesbos-Skyrosian?"

"Oh, yes," she said, walking forward, "although they may not know me."

"You're Madame Sardikos' companion," the tall man said dismissively. "The face is familiar."

"Yes," Madame Lesbos-Skyrosian said. "It's been nice talking to you, Mr. Tiebald, but we have to be running along."

"We have to meet some people at the Taverna Sounion," the short man added. "Nice meeting you, mister." He looked at Miss Melina for a moment, as if weighing whether or not to acknowledge her presence. At last simple humanity overcame class prejudice and he gave her a barely perceptible nod. Then they were gone.

"They left because of me," she said. "I'm sorry."

"I wasn't doing all that well without you. Can I buy you a drink?"

"No, thanks. Were you trying to persuade them to come over on our side?"

"Something like that." Karff finished his drink and picked up the check.

"You were doing the best you could, Mr. Thibalt. At least let me sign the check for you. I do it for the Madame all the time."

"Thank you. How do I call you? Miss Melina sounds a bit, well, pretentious. Like you were sixty-two instead of twenty-six." He knocked perhaps a decade off her age.

She flushed slightly. "Thank you. Call me Melina if you wish. Do you think the Skyrosi will come around for us?"

"Since you ask, no. All three of them are rigid, weak, and fearful. I expect they'll wind up telling General Delosian to go ahead, but be gentle about it."

Melina signed the check and they walked out into the hall. "What would you like to do?"

He looked down at her. I wonder what she wants, he thought.

And does it matter? "This is my first time in Enkomi. I'd like to look around, to see the city. Would you give me the grand tour?"

Enkomi was composed of irregular toruses stacked on the massive cable that supports the space elevator. Each torus was divided into four segments oriented north, east, south, and west, and decks, in the working section of the city, or levels, in the elite residential districts. The address of location was given by the torus number, counting upward, followed by the letter of the segment, followed by the deck number and room number. Karff, for instance, was staying in XVI-W02-2177, a guest room not far from Madame Sardikos' suite.

Local elevators moved within each segment of any given torus, maintaining its structural integrity. Express elevators moved between toruses in the interface between segments, touching any given segment on one deck only, usually adjacent to a police station. Not all express elevators stopped at all toruses. The express elevators opened into foyers which were within the interface and accessible to the segments on either side through airlocks.

There were gardens and aviaries, usually small, sculptured bubbles of atrium space, the avocation of some rich man or woman preserved as a memorial to his or her memory. The aquarium was for only the most delicate of tropical fish. There was a small mammal zoo. Art galleries were more common, requiring only hall space, lighting, and security. A popular site was the airlocks leading from the express elevators.

After eight centuries of history, Enkomi was undergoing a kind of seachange, into something rich and strange. Slowly it was becoming museumized, as the collections of the rich—often the residuum of a lifetime hobby—each occupying its finite volume, encroached upon the functional city. A machine slowly having parts of iron and brass replaced with gold.

There were also, of course, a profusion of entertainments. Clubs, pubs, theaters, restaurants, coffee houses, tavernas, dance halls, casinos, and sporting houses, a list by no means conclusive.

Karff and Melina toured an aviary, rode the elevators, passed through art galleries, rode the elevators, ate supper at a fine restaurant, rode the elevators, lost money at a casino, and rode the elevators.

They ended up at the lowest level.

"I've never been here before," she said. "This is where the water is purified, I think."

Karff stopped a guard. "Excuse me," he said, "the lady is giving me a tour of the city. What is there to see around here?"

"Trash disposal. The chief engineer's office is down the next corridor, on the right. Sir."

"Thank you," Karff said pleasantly.

The office was the only one open, and the chief engineer was sitting behind a glass partition. Startled, he stood when they knocked, and let them in.

"Good evening," Karff said. "Permit me to introduce myself. I am Mr. Thibalt and this is Miss Melina."

"How do ya do, sir. I'm Peter Strossos, the night shift head of maintenance. What can I do for ya?"

"Well, Mr. Strossos, Miss Melina was taking me on a tour of the city, and I thought that perhaps you might show us how the trash disposal works."

Surprised but nonethless pleased with the diversion, Strossos checked his watch. "We dump at twenty-five hundred hours. 'Bout half an hour from now. Come on, if ya want." They went down a long, curving corridor and a flight of stairs.

"What this is, is one of the main power plants. The power lines go up the express elevator shafts, and feed into the different toruses through airtight insulated seals. This is the East Generator. You can't go inside, because it's radioactive. The controls are six decks up, if ya want to see them."

"I don't think so," Miss Melina said. "After this I think we'll go home."

"Right," the engineer said. "Here ya are." They went through a door marked DO NOT ENTER in red letters, and found themselves in a large room with a smooth, sloping floor. The bottom of the floor was piled high with trash, old newspapers, bags, bottles, junk.

"This is the holding bin," Strossos said. "See, the city's trash is collected in little blue carts that go up and down the express elevators. They come here through those doors along the wall and dump the trash. Mostly it slides down on top of the trapdoor in the middle—ya can't see it because it's under the trash. What happens is that the trapdoor opens and lets the trash fall into the airlock underneath. Well, into the bin *in* the

105

airlock underneath. Then the trapdoor closes, and the airlock opens, and the bin tilts and the trash falls out."

"Down onto Ayios Sostis?"

"No, lady. The trash falls into the ocean, what part of it doesn't burn up in the atmosphere. See, *we* are moving east at about twenty-eight hundred kilometers per hour, relative the center of Malusia. And so is the trash. Now the surface of Malusia is only moving 'bout a thousand kph, so that by the time the trash gets down there—it's a ninety-eight-minute fall, at least, it's ninety-eight minutes till ya see the flash—it's about fourteen or fifteen hundred kilometers due east."

"That's very interesting, Mr. Strossos," Karff said. "How do you get in to the airlock under the trapdoor? I imagine *it* has to be maintained, too."

"The yellow and black door over there," the engineer said. Karff walked over to take a closer look.

"The pressure gauge says eight hundred millibars. Is it safe to enter?"

"I don't think I want to go in there, Mr. Thibalt," Melina said.

"It's safe," the engineer said. "Just bleed air in until it equalizes, and open the door. Inside a revolving door takes ya into the bin, but it won't turn until ya close the door behind you. A semiairlock. Ya want to go in, sir?"

"What's inside?"

"Just a walkway going around three sides of the bin. The reason the pressure is down in there is that the gaskets haven't been replaced for more than twenty years, and they leak."

Karff suddenly felt disinclined to go through the door. "Very interesting," he said. "I *would* like to watch the dump, if you don't mind."

"Let's go to the office, then. Ya can see more looking down, and watch the TV monitor to see the bin dumping."

They went up a spiral staircase and reached a little glass box with a big television screen. At midnight the trapdoor opened, and they watched the day's trash pour into the bin. Then it closed again, and they turned to the TV monitor. The airlock slowly opened, the bin slowly rotated, the trash slowly dumped, the bin slowly returned to position, and the airlock slowly closed.

"That's it," Strossos said.

"What do you do for excitement around here?" Karff asked.

"Once in a while a body turns up inside. Then we have to notify the police. Usually it's a naked lady—a crime of passion. The pros put the body in a trash bag and we never see it."

Chapter 12.

Flight from Malusia

ON THE ISS *Grand Duke Grossnickel*, the Grand Duke Sergius sat at a card table covered with green baize with the three senior members of the Imperial Household who were closest to him, his so-called inner circle.

Both sides vulnerable. Sergius, sitting South, held S: Q10xx, H: xxxx, D: A, C: Jxxx. North, in third position, opened one spade. East passed, and Sergius, counting his singleton diamond as 3 points, and promoting his queen–ten of spades from 2 to 3+ points, counted 11 points in his hand and rounded it up to 12, to bid three spades. The hand was passed out.

"Stretching it a little, *weren't* you," North said as the dummy went down. However, the cards broke right and he made three spades, with 20 points in high cards in the combined hands.

"Grossly overplayed," Sergius said, writing down the 90 part-score.

On the next hand, Sergius held S: QJ, H: AKxx, D: Qxxx, C: QJx. North opened the bidding with one no-trump, indicating 16 to 18 points. Sergius counted 15 points in high cards, so that if his partner had 18, the combined hands totaled 33 points, the minimum for a small slam. Sergius looked at the part-score, subtracted 1 point for the doubleton queen of spades, and passed.

While North was making five overtricks at one no-trump, Count Franz-Otto handed Sergius a message.

"So," Sergius said. "The Rebel Fleet has arrived." He checked his watch. "About an hour ago. How should we proceed, do you think?"

"Decamp," East said. "We've discussed the point often enough. As I recall, we even settled on the optimum line of departure."

"Of course," Sergius said.

"We should have left days ago," West said. "How does it happen that we are still here?"

"Ah"—Sergius fingered his magnificent mustache—"it seems to me that General Francisco Bloyer might have had something to do with that. He was, as I recall, the chief advocate of conquering Malusia. We sent a scouting party in, and when they reported back affirmatively, this same Bloyer, blowing hot and cold, found some pretext to send them back again."

"Charming fellow, Bloyer," North said. "Simply charming. Do you trust the slimy son of a bitch?"

Sergius shook his leonine head. "I'm afraid not."

"It *does* look like he was stalling our departure until the Rebel Fleet arrived," East said. "What shall we do about *him*?"

"Remove him with the utmost delicacy," Sergius said. "Admiral Heydrich will, I am sure, be pleased to cooperate in the project." He ripped off the bridge score, and wrote on the back: "Arrest Gen. Bloyer's aide, Lt. Col. Schrader, immediately on the charge of treason. /s/ Sergius, Regent." The others initialed off on it.

"Will that be sufficient?" North asked. "I would have thought that at least two or three of Bloyer's creatures ought to be taken."

"Perhaps," Sergius said agreeably. "Whom did you have in mind?"

There was a pause.

"Excuse me," Count Franz-Otto said, "but Colonel Himmelreich might make an excellent example."

"Yes," North said. "His whole career has hung on his connection with Bloyer, and he won't be missed."

"I agree," East said. "Arrest those two and leave Bloyer twisting slowly, slowly in the wind."

Sergius tore off another sheet from the scorepad and wrote off Colonel Himmelreich. "So much for Bloyer. A hangman is never popular, and we can settle his fate at our leisure."

"Very good, sir," Count Franz-Otto said, taking the second arrest order. "What about Colonel Karff's group on Malusia?"

"It would take two days to return them to the fleet," North said. "I think we must cast them off."

"True enough," Sergius said. "If we are here more than another three or four hours I am going to be extremely annoyed.

However, we shall send them an affectionate farewell." He picked up the deck and began to shuffle the blue-backed cards as North dealt the red ones. "Check the file, Count. It seems to me that there is a contingency memo we can use."

"Very good, sir. Will that be all?"

"Just a moment." Sergius took back the arrest order for Lieutenant Colonel Schrader and added up the scores on its back.

Chapter 13.
Karff's Retreat

THE BEDSIDE PHONE rang and rang again. Karff pushed himself up on one elbow and picked up the phone.

"Hanh?" he said.

"Is that you, Thibalt?"

"Unh-hnh," he said, turning on the night-table lamp. "What is it, Judith?"

"We have word from Sergius that the Rebel Fleet"—she used the Imperiales expression—"has arrived. He's pulling out. By now he probably *has* pulled out."

"Right." Karff sat up and scratched his hairy chest. "What do you want me to do about it?"

"Come home. We have a coded message marked for your eyes only, and I'm dying of curiosity."

"I'll think about it." On the couch a white, wraithlike figure with long hair of indeterminate color pushed off the blanket and stumbled toward the bathroom. "I'll disengage here and get back as soon as possible. I'll give you a call first."

"I miss you, Thibalt."

"Take care of yourself, Judith. I miss you, too." As he hung up, Melina was being sick in the bathroom.

The sooner I get back to the transporter the better, Karff thought, rubbing his face with his hand. Scouting Enkomi is strictly useless at this point, unless I mean 'totally stupid.' Melina sounded acutely nauseated.

"Rinse out your mouth with water, Melina. You'll feel better." The reply was inaudible, a dry heave with a question mark. He went into the bathroom and gave her a glass of water. "Rinse out your mouth."

She did, resting her forearms on the toilet bowl. "I feel awful."

"Again," Karff said, offering her more water. She spat a mouthful into the bowl and swallowed a little.

"You're naked!"

"Also I don't have any clothes on," Karff agreed. He flushed the toilet, then helped her stand. "Neither do you."

"I don't?" She looked down at herself. "I guess not. What happened?"

"On the way back from the trash dump we stopped at a pub."

"The Clown and Garter—I had a drink."

"You had more than one, Melina. Do you remember the tattoo parlor? You *insisted* on going in."

"Tattoo parlor?"

"Look at your lower belly." She looked down and touched the red and black design on her creamy skin.

"What is it?" she said. "I don't have my contacts on."

"A black skull and crossbones with a wreath of scarlet oak leaves," he replied. "You really liked my buttons."

"Aiii! Ai! Ai!" she wailed. He put his hand over her mouth, not hard. She got hold of herself, and he let go. "Then what?" she asked hopelessly.

"We stopped at the Mirror Blue and you had a few more. Then you invited yourself in here for a nightcap."

"I'm *tattooed*," she said. "I didn't *really* invite myself into your room, did I?"

"You really did," Karff said. "Then while I was trying to figure out how to make coffee, you said, 'Let's play doctor!' and when I looked up you'd taken it all off." She looked stricken. "Then you kissed me with great ardor and passed out."

"Oh, no," she said urgently, as if denying it would make it unhappen. "Oh, no, oh, no, oh, no!" She went into the bedroom. "My clothes! Where are my clothes?! My clothes aren't here!!" When Karff came out of the bathroom she was looking under the bed.

"Hey Melina, I hung them in the closet."

"What did you do with *me*?"

"You I put on the sofa and covered with a blanket."

"I'm tattooed," she said softly and began to weep. Karff sat down on the bed and held her, rocking her back and forth.

"There, there, Melina," he said soothingly. I don't suppose

a late start out of here is going to be all that critical, he thought, and if it is, that's just too damn bad.

General Delosian slumped in his high-backed leather chair and rubbed his eyes. His desk, usually immaculate, was littered with paper. His grooming, usually impeccable, was lax.

"I apologize for the actions of my fellows," Gregor Naxos said. "The Great Holders of Naxos unfortunately feel that Madame Sardikos' plan must be tried."

"Don't apologize," Delosian said wearily. "You did all you could. How long can we keep matters from coming to a vote?"

"Eh? We can stall for a few days." Gregor Naxos grinned. "I'll tell 'em Delos is coming around! *They'll* wait!"

"How long?"

"A week. Ten days at the outside. Madame Sardikos won't put up with much more."

"I'll take it. My luck just might pull me through." He straightened some of the papers on his desk. "You know this marks the end of our power, of course."

"The popular phrase is 'civilization as we know it,'" Gregor said. "And yes, *I* know it, and so do some of the others—my fellow Great Holders who switched to Sardikos."

Delosian sat up and straightened his tie. "Hey, if they *knew*, then why?—"

"What can I say?" The burly man spread his hands. "The logic of our position sometimes requires painful choices."

"Maybe we *should* have built a second space elevator," Delosian mused.

Gregor Naxos shook his head. "Play differently, lose differently. Madame Sardikos took it, you know, when she asked what a government was that we should fear it so. Some fool gave her the stock answer, and she said, 'Is that more evil than slaying hungry people for trying to feed themselves?'"

"I said, 'Nuke them'... perhaps I should have been a little more tactful," Delosian conceded, "a little less explicit." He shook his head. "Well, what's done is done." He turned his chair and glanced at the banner displaying the Delian coat of arms behind his desk, a shield, argent, bearing a dragon's head erased, gules, the whole set on a field of dark blue. "I do not forget to smash the state," he said sadly, "but there appears to be no way to keep it from springing into unwholesome life."

113

After Gregor Naxos had left, the general called his chief of operations. "Hello, Marko. Do we have a line on Thibalt's group yet?"

"Funny you should ask, sir. We got a break early this morning. A call to his room from someone named Judith. We traced it—the call came into Enkomi from Malusiopolis. We have the number and the address, but the call *originated* from a ship-to-shore phone in the vicinity of Ayios Sostis."

"Do you have that number?"

"No, sir. However, we have tapped the Moptown number, and if and when Mr. Thibalt calls back, we'll get it. No matter *where* he calls from."

"Good." Delosian turned over a piece of paper. "That *might* be sufficient. And if it isn't, what have we lost? You knew that Mr. Thibalt, poor fellow, asked Madame Sardikos for permission to go to Ayios Sostis?" A smile creased his leathery face. "The good Madame said no, of course. However, Mr. Thibalt strikes me as a resourceful chap. If he were to vanish, who could doubt that he simply went home?"

Karff buttoned his burgundy silk shirt over his gevlar vest, tucking the shirttail into his white silk trousers. The white-on-white silk tie he knotted carefully and secured with a white pearl tie tack. Looking good, he thought confidently; perhaps a little charm will persuade Madame Sardikos to let me head back for a few days in Ayios Sostis. Or perhaps not.

There was a knock at the door. The spy-hole showed a short, stocky man in a messenger's uniform holding a package with a clipboard underneath it. Karff opened the door, and the man handed him the clipboard and a pencil.

"Sign here, please."

Karff took the pencil and the man pulled a stainless steel revolver with a silencer from his pants pocket and fired four shots into Karff's chest.

Karff heard the first two shots and felt the double blow slam into him. He raised his head very slowly, dropping the pencil and clipboard, which began to drift toward the floor, and pushed forward from his left foot as he slowly, slowly raised his right hand. The third shot hit him on the sternum, just above his tie tack. He put his weight on his right foot as his right hand turned edgewise to strike and his left hand reached for the revolver in the short man's right hand. The fourth shot struck him over the heart. Then his left foot came up and caught the man in the groin, and as it recoiled, his right hand chopped into the side of the man's neck. The blow was intended to kill, but the neck was unexpectedly muscular and didn't break. The left hand slid over the pistol and seized hand and wrist, pulling them forward and away. As the man started to go down, Karff hit him a second time with the right hand, again chopping into the neck.

Karff took the pistol from limp fingers and hurled the man into the room. He kicked the clipboard inside, and when he closed the door, it pushed the gaily wrapped package into the room.

As Karff picked up the package, Melina came out of the bathroom in her black negligee. "What happened?" She put her hands over her mouth.

"A little slash and splash," Karff replied. Blood stained the pistol and the package. He looked at his left palm, which was wet. "I cut my hand on the front sight, I think. Get dressed!" Wide-eyed, she did as she was told. His voice of command was quite as peremptory as that of Madame Sardikos, and she was trained to obedience.

The package, when he opened it, held a large trash bag. On the floor, the man in the messenger's uniform stirred. Do I need to ask him anything? Karff thought. Not really—besides, he's a pro. Even if he knew anything, there wouldn't be time to make him talk. He put the silenced pistol behind the man's ear and delivered the coup de grace. Then he put him in the trash bag, wrapped a handkerchief around his left hand, and closed the bag, winding the corners of the mouth into ears, and tying the ears in a double knot. He moved the bag into the foyer by the front door and knocked on the bathroom door.

"I'm not ready, yet," Melina said.

"Hey, sweetheart, I'd like to bandage my hand."

"Oh." She opened the door wearing only her bra and panties, and bandaged his hand. The cut had bled freely, but it wasn't deep. He kissed her with genuine appreciation.

"You'd better change, too," she said. He looked at himself on the door mirror. Bloodstains on his pants, powder burns and a bullet hole in his tie, bullet holes in his shirt.

"I'm not presentable," he agreed. He changed into a white-on-white silk pinstripe suit he hadn't yet worn, putting on a ruffled emerald-green silk shirt over his vest, knotting a white silk tie with a white silk dragon. Then the matching green handkerchief and skullcap. He wiped off the stainless steel pistol with his shot-up burgundy shirt and put it in his pocket. Then he checked the corridor. Empty.

He dragged the trash bag outside and saw the messenger's four-wheel freight cart sitting against the wall. How convenient, he thought, and put the body on it. He rolled down the hall to the stairwell, where there was a trash container on the landing. Picking up the body, he heaved it into the container with a grunt. The pistol he broke open. The six cartridges were spent; the messenger must have carried the pistol with an empty under the hammer. The pistol went into the trash also. The freight cart he left in the hall.

Fine, he thought. All the tactical loose ends are taken care of. Now we have only strategic loose ends, namely, How do I get out of Enkomi? When he went back into the room, Melina was dressed and waiting for him.

"What was that all about?" she asked.

"The man on the floor tried to kill me. But I don't know why. Here." He handed her four flattened 8.02-millimeter slugs he had taken out of his burgundy shirt.

"What should I do with them?" she asked.

"Put them on a charm bracelet," Karff said. "That's four times the man tried to kill me and failed. Tonight I'll show you the bruises if you like."

"They have a cloth pattern on the end," she said. "Your bullet-proof vest really works?" He nodded. "What happened to the man?"

"I sent him on his way. If I don't get out of Enkomi, I may wind up following him."

"You *can't* leave Enkomi. The Madame has forbidden it."

"If I stay here I'm dead. The next time, I'll catch the slugs in the back of the head."

"I'll help you any way I can," she said, "but I can't get you out of Enkomi. The security on the space elevators is *very* tight, and it isn't only Madame Sardikos, either."

"Right," Karff said. "That would be the logical place to watch for me." He pulled at his nose with his thumb and forefinger.

"Enkomi is a very old city," she said. "There are lots and lots of places to hide."

"Do you know them?"

"No." She shook her head. "Only from reading books."

"I haven't even read the books," he said gently. Hell, he thought, I can't hide, I can't run, and I can't fight. What to do? "Why don't we go out and get some breakfast? I'm sure I'll think better after I've had a cup of coffee."

They took the elevator down to the Sardikos Cafeteria, an enormous, institutional, impersonal food-processing center, gleaming with stainless steel and pastel-green plastic. Arriving at the end of the morning rush, Karff found they were out of home-friend potatoes, so he accepted grits with his fried eggs, and toast and coffee. He found a table for two against the wall.

"Look," Melina said, "why don't you tell Madame Sardikos so she can protect you?"

"She can't," he said.

"She would so!"

"Hey, Melina, I'm not putting down the Madame. It can't be *done*. She can put me in an egg, and the egg in a box, and the box in the deep blue sea, and if they want me, they will, by God, *get* me. I used to be in the business. I *know*. And that, of course, assumes it wasn't the *Madame* out to get me."

"Oh! Oh! You are utterly *awful*!"

He shrugged and took a sip of coffee.

"If you aren't going to ask Madame Sardikos to protect you, what *are* you going to do?" Melina said at last.

"Have another cup of coffee," Karff said, waving to the waitress. "After that, I'll make a phone call."

"Do you have a plan?" she asked.

"No. Only an idea." The waitress refilled his cup, and he stirred it absently, watching the steam rise over the dark liquid. "Wait here," he said at last, "I'll be right back."

"Where are you going?"

"The phone booth is right over there," he said, pointing with his thumb. "Don't take your eyes off me, all right?"

She nodded and bit her lip as he stood up.

Ildenhagen answered the phone.

"Look, this is what I need done . . ."

* * *

Mitropolous and Kohnos, New & Used Spacesuits, Retrofitting Our Specialty, Repairs Done On The Premises, III-W17-1241, was a deep room with a balcony tucked between the freight elevators and the space elevator docks. Its window displayed spacesuits, helmets, and all manner of accessory equipment.

The salesman wore a checkered jacket and a heavy black mustache, and because there was no business he came over smiling, just as if these two upper-class tourists were real customers.

"Good morning, sir and madame," he said, "may I be of assistance to you?"

"Yes, actually," Karff said. "I need a spacesuit. Tonight. Can you outfit me?"

"Ah—yes. Yes, of course, sir. We may not have a wide assortment on hand. How much did you wish to spend?"

Karff reached into his pocket and felt his roll of bills. "That will depend on what I have to buy. What have you got?"

The salesman took his measurements and consulted the computer on his desk.

"Nothing fancy," he said at last. "We have six or seven suits you could wear. Standard maintenance models, mostly in fair to good condition. We have one 'like new,' but it doesn't have magnetic grapples."

"Let's see it."

The salesman pushed a button and a collection of spacesuits hung on a conveyor belt rolled past. "This is it. New, it would run you 6,990 dolars. I can let you have it for 5,990." Karff didn't say anything. "Perhaps 5,500, but *that* is as low as I can go."

"*I* could go 5,000," Karff said.

"You're paying cash?"

Karff nodded. "Dirty old money. Half now, half when I pick it up before close of business today."

"Yes, sir." Karff counted out twenty-five 100-dolar bills, and the salesman rang them up.

"Very good, sir. Will you want any accessory equipment?"

"Strobe lights front and rear. And a carrier, of course."

"The carrier comes with the suit, sir. We have five sizes of strobe lights in white, and three in red and green. Very reasonably priced, too, sir, if I may say so." He led Karff and

Melina over to the display case, and Karff picked out the largest white strobe.

"Two of them, right?"

"Yes, sir." The salesman raised his eyebrows but said nothing. The customer is always right.

While Melina sat in the front of the shop leafing through old copies of *Spacesuit Repair* and *Illustrated Spacesuits*, Karff put on the suit and had it fitted. After the inner pressure suit was in position, a fitter put on the outer girdle, which made it possible to move around. When he had fitted the girdle to his satisfaction, he inflated the suit to approximate conditions in space.

"Not much to do here," the fitter said. "Come by in a couple of hours, and we take a second fitting. The girdle doesn't always sit right the first time. We check it for leaks then, also."

"What about the strobes?"

"They'll be mounted, sir."

Karff nodded and went out for a leisurely lunch with Melina in a local cafe. When he came back, the suit was ready to go. No leaks, no bulges, no wrinkles, and the strobe lights worked. He put the suit in the carrier, a bulky blue case on casters, and rented a hotel room a few decks down.

"Now what?" Melina asked.

"Now we have about ten hours to kill," Karff said. "As soon as I write a short letter, I shall help you kill it."

"I don't know whether I should let you—"

"Wouldn't you like to make love when you weren't deathly ill? Pull down your skirt and contemplate your tattoo for a few minutes."

Much later that evening he walked her down to the express elevator, the spacesuit carrier trailing along behind him.

"I'm in trouble," he said quietly, "and I'm trying to work my way out as best I know how. You can help." He handed her the letter. "See that Madame Sardikos gets this. Will you do that for me?"

"What is it?" she asked.

He smiled. "A letter." A way to remove you gracefully from the scene of my exit, he thought. Why be messy or brutal if you don't have to? Bad enough that you're going to tell her you love her when you kiss her good-bye.

After she was gone, he went down to where the trash was

dumped, and in one of the side rooms he put on the spacesuit, leaving his clothes in the carrier.

He went through the yellow-and-black-striped door and closed it behind him. The revolving door moved stiffly, but it moved, and he went out on the catwalk. After a few minutes, the roof opened and the day's trash came pouring into the bin below. Then the roof closed, and the airlock slowly began to open. When the bin started to turn for the dump, he turned on the strobe lights. I have had more brilliant ideas, he thought grimly. Well, if Stavo *doesn't* catch me with FAD-200, I'm going out in the proverbial blaze of glory. He swung over the rail, and as the last of the trash spilled out, he let go, dropping through the airlock with strobe lights flashing.

Chapter 14.
Pattern for Conquest, Rebel

ABOARD THE *Grendlsmöder*, the flagship of the POUM wing of the FURDS-controlled Popular Front, Commissioner P. Joseph Fouché removed a scented cigarette from his platinum case and held it between his thumb and forefinger. Three admirals offered him a light. He drew on his cigarette, then took his seat at the head of the conference table.

"The Imperial dogs ran as I feared they would," he said, exhaling blue smoke. "Can we pursue them?"

"Yes, Mr. Commissioner," said an admiral with an eye-patch. "After we rededicate the drives. Catching them..." He shrugged.

"You all say that," Fouché snapped. "Rededicate the drives! Rededicate the drives! Where is the drives' revolutionary consciousness, eh? We are forging a new Man, why not a new Machine, as well?"

"These machines were all built by the Empire," a bald admiral said. "Mistreat them, they don't work. Shoot them, we don't go home."

"We can't go home *anyway* without destroying the Imperial Fleet," Fouché said grimly.

"Yes, Mr. Commissioner, but we cannot pursue them immediately at this time," the one-eyed admiral replied.

"Where did they run to?"

"To KCC-10771, Mr. Commissioner, an unfruited star about two weeks' travel from here, pretty much straight out. From there, they have a number of choices."

"Then prepare to depart for KCC-107—that star. Do it *now!*"

"Yes, Mr. Commissioner," the bald admiral said. "I would be remiss in my duty if I did not inform you that we will lose a tenth of the fleet en route."

Fouché blew smoke in his face.

"It is also very possible," the admiral continued, "that the Imperial Fleet will come back *here*. Malusia is the logical place for them to establish a base, after all. Follow them back immediately, we will lose *half* the fleet."

"And the half that makes it will arrive piecemeal," the one-eyed admiral added, "so that the Imperial Fleet will destroy them in detail. What then, Mr. Commissioner?"

"Don't bait him, Admiral," the Deputy Commissioner asked. "Joseph, my son, suppose the Imperial Fleet had gone when we arrived. What would you have done then?"

"Ahh, Padre . . ." Fouché flicked ash on the carpet. "Then we wouldn't have known where they ran to. I suppose we would have settled in here to keep them from coming back."

"Why not do it now, Joseph? The chances are excellent that they *will* come back here, especially compared to the chances of catching them on the run."

"We can't go back without them."

"Or without some notable accomplishment. Such as the conquest of Malusia." The Deputy Commissioner turned to the admiral. "You were showing me the intelligence summary of the local system. The Board might be interested."

The one-eyed admiral opened his briefcase and spread a map on the conference table. "This is the Malusian system. The local civilization consists of a dozen or so space habitats, and several cities on the planet Malusia. Connected"—he placed a glossy photograph on the table—"by a working space elevator."

"A working space elevator?" Fouché examined the photograph. "This place is a piece of cake. The Imperial Fleet— how could it *not* return here?"

"They might—" a third admiral began.

"And then again they might not." The deputy cut him off. "How often must I tell you, think positively."

"Interesting," Fouché said, putting out his cigarette. "Very interesting. I am convinced. The Imperial dogs will return here. Therefore, we must conquer this place, and hold it against their return."

"I agree, Joseph," his deputy said. "What do you military men think?"

One-eye looked at his fellows. "An excellent plan. We are in total agreement, Mr. Commissioner."

"Good," Fouché said. "You had damn well better be. Now, then. How shall we proceed?"

The admirals stood over the map. "This configuration bears a striking resemblance to Lyonsk," the bald one said.

"Yes," the third admiral said. "We could begin here or *here*"—he jabbed the map with a finger—"equally well. What is your pleasure, Mr. Commissioner?"

"This one," said Fouché, placing a nicotine-stained finger on Naxos.

Chapter 15.
Imperial Rear Guard

THE 16,090-KILOMETER fall—not a free fall, but one carefully regulated—came to an end 9,982 meters above sea level, 236.22 kilometers northwest of Ayios Sostis, as Transporter *42210* made the catch with Captain Ildenhagen piloting, Sergeant Stavo manning the FAD-200, and Sergeant Arcziari on the cargo bay deck to ensure against slippage. Karff turned off the strobe lights that had helped Stavo spot him then came aboard, shaking hands all around. Schmitt had baked a cake and iced some champagne. Finally Karff went into his suite, stacked the space-suit in a chair, and showered and shaved, reestablishing his presence in the antiseptically neat bathroom.

Feeling refreshed, Karff put on his class-A blacks and went to the Bridge, where Captain Ildenhagen was holding the con. "I understand the Regent sent me a message."

"Yep." Ildenhagen put down her coffee cup. "Here you are." The message was in the form of an interactive videodisc, and Karff took it into the communications room, where he put it on the machine. The screen lit up with a test pattern.

"This message is classified *Secret*," a clear mechanical voice said, "and is intended for Senior Colonel S.T. Karff, only. Will you identify yourself, please?"

"I am Colonel Karff."

"Very good, sir. Will you please repeat the phrase 'Two twin-screw steel cruisers?'" Voice comparisons were necessary but not sufficient. A tape might recite an identification. The query for an unexpected phrase was a safeguard, and if it failed to yield positive results, the videodisc would be erased.

"Two twin-screw steel scruisers—cruisers!"

"Very good, sir." The television screen came to life, panning in on the Grand Duke Sergius sitting at his desk, where he looked directly at the camera and gave the military salute.

124

"In the name of the Holy Human Empire," he began, and Karff came to involuntary attention, every hair struggling to stand on end, "and in the name of Prince Fredy Maria Gustavos von Portales und Halberschlange, whom we have the honor to serve as Regent, we salute you.

"The Imperial Fleet must now depart from Malusia, fleeing the vastly superior Rebel forces which have pursued us here. We believe that the Rebels, motivated by implacable hatred, will conquer Malusia and seek to use it as a base from which to continue that pursuit.

"You are hereby appointed to the position of Commander of the Imperial Malusian Expeditionary Force.

"It is your duty and honor to resist the Rebel forces by any and every means, with all the force at your command, to the utmost limits of your strength.

"Senior Colonel Saloman Thibalt Karff, you have served the Empire faithfully and well, and since we will never meet again in this life, we must now tell you that those services have been deeply appreciated and inadequately honored." Sergius took a red leather box from his desk and opened it, the camera panning in on the box to show a maltese cross of black iron bearing the Imperial Crown over crossed swords in enameled gold. "From this moment forward, you are a Knight of the Empire, Third Class!" The camera backed off to show Sergius fingering his mustache and smiling a trifle apologetically. "First and Second Class, as I expect you know, being reserved for the Imperial Household.

"Good luck, Sir Karff, and may God assist you in the honorable discharge of your new duties." Sergius stood and once again saluted, as the camera panned backward to show the picture of Prince Fredy and the Imperial Battle Ensign. Then the stirring music of the "Degradero" sounded, and Karff's eyes welled over with tears.

"End of message," the mechanical voice announced. "A small package was sent along with the videotape. Please be sure to ask about it, Sir Karff."

Karff wiped his eyes with his handkerchief and blew his nose. When he could finally talk, he went out on the Bridge and asked Ildenhagen if there had been anything else for him.

"There *was*, you know," she said, tilting back her head to look down her nose at him. "Here it is." She handed him a metal cylinder stenciled with the Imperial seal. He unscrewed the end and grasped the loop of blue tape that fell out, pulling the tape to extract the cylinder of flexible foam that filled the metal can. Once the foam cylinder was free, he peeled off the tape to reveal that the cylinder was split. Inside the foam packing was a red leather box. And inside the red leather box was the Order of Knight of the Holy Human Empire, Third Class, inscribed with his name, registration number, and date.

In the east, the Malusian sky was beginning to lighten with the new day.

"The last thing Thibalt told me was that I should give you this letter," Miss Melina said, handing it across the coffee table to her mistress. "He said it was important, and that was the last time I saw him." Madame Sardikos took the letter and slit it open with her thumbnail.

"Hmmph," she said, reading. "He thanks me for my hospitality. A bread-and-butter note."

"That's *all*, Madame?"

"See for yourself. You didn't think he was asking me for your hand, did you?" Melina blushed, but took the letter. "You did! You *did* think so! You are an incurable sentimentalist and romantic, and I'm a half-witted old fool for letting you out at night!"

"No, Madame. I am grateful to you for the experience." Melina put the letter back in its envelope.

"Good. Sexual repression can be overdone, you know." Madame Sardikos sat back on the striped divan and fingered her pearl necklace. "Going back a little—after you heard the ruckus at the door, you came out of the bathroom and saw the messenger lying on the floor. What happened to him?"

"I don't know. Thibalt told me to get dressed, and I never saw him again."

Madame Sardikos nodded. "I see," she said at last. "The package that Mr. Thibalt was holding—what was in it?"

"The package . . ." Melina closed her eyes, concentrating. "There were bloodstains on it. From his cut hand. And the wrapping was on the floor when I came out afterwards, but I never saw what was in it."

"Probably a trash bag," the old woman said. The door chimes sounded. "Would you get the door, please?"

Melina ushered Dr. John Naxos-Limnion and Gregor Naxos into the living room. Madame Sardikos looked up from the green-striped divan.

"Please be seated, gentlemen," she said coldly. "What can I do for you?"

"A small favor," Gregor Naxos said, clasping his large hands together. "Could you perhaps arrange for us a meeting with your friend, Mr. Thibalt?"

"Whatever for?"

"There's a chance..." Gregor began and fell silent.

"We have just learned that there is a fleet of warships standing off Naxos," Dr. John Naxos-Limnion said, his dark eyebrows accentuating the concern in his dark eyes. "At the last report they were demanding that a surrender be negotiated. We thought that your Mr. Thibalt might know something about them."

"Fleet? *What* fleet?" Madame Sardikos was genuinely startled.

Gregor shrugged. "We have no idea," he said, "that's why we'd like to talk to *him*."

"He isn't available," Madame Sardikos said. "Yesterday morning he had a run-in with an assassin, and has since made himself scarce." The two men exchanged glances, and Gregor sighed.

"General Delosian is sometimes a trifle hasty," Dr. John conceded. "He survived?"

"The assassin?" Madame Sardikos smiled. "I wouldn't know. I *told* you that Mr. Thibalt made himself scarce. When last seen he was surviving."

"When and where was that, please?" Gregor asked. Melina looked at the Madame, who nodded.

"Last night, a little before midnight," Melina said. "We were near the express elevators on Three-W—not far from the old docks. He had a spacesuit in a carrier with him."

"He could play hidey-go for *years* down there," Gregor said. "Especially if he has connections."

"So put out a reward," the old woman said. "How badly do you want to talk to him?"

"I don't know." Dr. John seemed exasperated. "If he's connected down at the docks, the chances are he *isn't* connected with this fleet that's sitting off Naxos. We'll put out a reward on the assumption that he's a stranger."

"The other thing, Madame Sardikos"—Gregor leaned forward in his gold and white chair—"is that we would like to defer the question of producing food on Malusia until we have dealt with these people."

"What people?"

"The people in the fleet. They identify themselves as the FURDS Fleet, POUM Faction, without ever saying what FURDS or POUM is."

"*Can* we deal with the threat?" she asked.

"We must," Dr. John replied. "So, naturally, we will. Please defer your motion to permit the production of food on Malusia."

"Are you still spooked by a big shaggy government emerging out of the swamps of Malusia?" Madame Sardikos asked. Dr. John nodded. "I see. Tell me, then—are you more scared of the government that our own people might make or of the government that the FURDS/POUM people might impose?"

"*Any* government is evil," Gregor Naxos replied solemnly.

"It isn't a matter of choosing," Dr. John said. "They have to be stopped."

"I see." Madame Sardikos paused briefly. "Well. If we lose, it won't matter, will it? I shall defer calling the question until this strange fleet has been chased off or destroyed or until—"

"Until *what*?" Gregor Naxos asked.

Madame Sardikos sat back on the green-and-white-striped divan. "Until Naxos surrenders, darling."

Chapter 16.
Rear Guard Action, Enkomi

"SPIESLINGER SURE DIDN'T bust his hump putting *this* together," Karff growled, tossing the Mamnu–Imperiales dictionary onto the glass-topped table in his suite. "What does it have, ten thousand entries?"

"Yes, sir," Sergeant Stavo said. "Something like that. This here's the list of supplemental terms you wanted." He handed over several pages typed in two columns. "I wrote them up, and Judith translated and typed them. In alphabetical order, except for the afterthoughts on the last page. And words of mechanically simulated telekinesis from *ablonging* to *zybchik*."

"Another two hundred words, you think?"

"The afterthoughts bring it to two hundred twenty-four, sir. Now what?"

"Cut and paste. I want it in alphabetical order before we dupe it. How is it going with that little copier we rented?"

Stavo shrugged. "Slow, but we're getting clean copy. We finished *My System* by Nimzovitch, and we're starting on his *MST Praxis*. That leaves the other seven volumes to go."

"Hell and damnation! The war is going to be over and done with before we get those mothers copied! Do you need all nine?"

"Yes, sir, Colonel Sir Karff, sir," Stavo said. "Out of more than a thousand books, textbooks, and manuals in my library box, I picked these. I would rather *add* to them than subtract."

"All right. Yes. You need all nine. Ten with the dictionary. Can't we get them done faster?"

"The little copier is slow, sir—"

"We couldn't bring a big, fast copier on board," Karff agreed, "but this simply will not *do*!"

* * *

A few minutes before closing time, the night manager in Fast Edie's Copying Service looked up in annoyance.

"We're closed, sir," she said. Arcziari grinned and said nothing. He just leaned on the counter in his black battle dress with the short machine gun slung over his shoulder. Then Stavo and Detana came through the back door she had just locked. Stavo was carrying his reader and the two books they had run off on the small copier, and the dictionary, and the books from his library that were going to be copied. Detana was pushing a hand truck and carrying a short machine gun slung across his chest.

"We're *closed*!" she insisted as Karff walked in and closed the door behind them.

"I hope that's negotiable, ma'am," he said as he locked the door. "We have some overtime here for you."

"I pay the A.S.V.P. for protection," she said. "The sticker is right there on the doorway! Now *git*!"

"I'm impressed," Karff said. "We need this job done to-night—fifty-four thousand pages—and we'll pay time-and-a-half. If you help us. Make a fuss, we'll tie you up and try to figure out how to work these complicated machines all by our thumb-fingered selves."

"Don't," she said, "I'll help. Can I call home to say a big rush job came in?" Karff nodded. As she reached for the phone, Arcziari snapped open his knife and began to clean his fingernails. She looked at Karff.

"Go ahead," he said. "He won't touch you without the word from me."

They left early the next morning. Edie totaled all the counters and wrote up a bill for 5,692.40 dolars.

"That's straight time," she said wearily.

"Including the binding?" Karff asked. She nodded. He took out his wallet and counted out six 1,000-dolar bills. "Time." Then he counted out three more. "Time and a half."

"You have some change coming."

"Keep the change, ma'am," Karff said. Then Detana opened the door and Arcziari and Stavo pushed the heavily loaded hand truck out into the aisle. Overhead, the glass roof of Ayios Sostis was filtering a ghostly half-light into the atrium on the other side of the aisle. The early risers gave the black uniformed

130

crew a wide berth until they reached the elevator. On the elevator were two blue-gray uniformed Ayios Sostis Volunteer Police toting short machine guns. One young and tall, one older and fat. There was a sudden restrained motion as four short machine guns were brought to port arms. Karff and Stavo, careful to keep out of the line of fire, rolled the hand truck onto the elevator.

"Good morning," Karff said pleasantly. "What can we do for you?"

"What outfit are you with?" the young policeman asked. "I don't recognize the uniforms."

"The Imperial Gestapo," Karff said.

"Union Goons? I don't like the sound of it. What are you up to?"

"Underraising the government," Karff said. "Any objections?"

The older policeman slung his machine gun. "No, sir. Just as long as you aren't drunk and disorderly."

Karff turned to Detana and Arcziari. "Sling arms, Sergeant," he said and repeated the order in Imperiales. Arcziari slung his machine gun. The older policeman said something to his partner, who slung his weapon, and Detana then slung his without orders and stepped aboard the elevator. Stavo pushed the button for the top level and the doors closed.

"Underraising the government is dry work," Karff said pleasantly, "and *most* of the time it is very quiet."

"Very good, sir," the older policeman said. He held the door as they rolled the cart off. Karff grinned and gave him the thumbs-up sign.

"Viva la Bureaucracy!" he said as the doors closed.

They rolled across the top of Ayios Sostis, smelling the ocean and feeling the morning breeze as it began to freshen in the new day. Concrete and stainless steel and hazy glass overhead. Ayios Sostis was almost as much a habitat as any structure in space. Air and water were present in abundance, but the space elevator was an umbilical cord binding it to the sky.

They crossed a footbridge and took a freight elevator down to where their boat was waiting for them. Karff rang the buzzer several times until the little captain got up and let them aboard. They drove out to the rendezvous point, and Captain Ildenhagen brought the transporter down to rope-ladder level. Sergeant

Stavo scrambled up the ladder, and the books went up via the FAD-200.

"Eh, sir," the little captain said as Karff paid him off. "We've 'ad inquiries about you, you know." Karff raised an eyebrow. "One of the Delian groups. They wanted to know about that ship-to-shore phone we don't 'ave anymore. What ought I to tell 'em?"

"They're coming back?"

"Yes, sir. This afternoon, they said."

"Hmm." Karff pulled his nose between his thumb and forefinger. "Tell them that Mr. Thibalt is back in Ayios Sostis." He turned to Arcziari standing at the stern of the boat. "Have Stavo send down a package of books, would you, Sergeant?" Arcziari yelled up, and after a few moments, a package of nine books and a dictionary tied up with string came gently down to the deck. Karff handed them to the little captain.

"See that the Delians get these," he said. "Tell them they go to General Delosian."

Then he clambered aboard the transporter, followed by Detana and Arcziari, and vanished into the morning sky.

Melina walked into Madame Sardikos' drawing room with an opened package, which she placed on the inlaid sideboy, beside the cut-crystal decanters. "It is books only, Madame. The guards made fun of me for being apprehensive."

"You told them you were protecting *my* well-being, I trust." The old lady picked up the top book on the stack. "This appears to be a dictionary, Melina. Translate a little for me, if you please."

Melina examined the dictionary. "Around the seal on the cover," she began, the seal being a skull and crossbones in a wreath of oak leaves, "is inscribed 'Imperial Gestapo Press.'"

"Imperial Union Goons Press?"

"No, Madame. Here *gestapo* is defined as 'One; A secret state police force noted for its exemplary conduct, patriotic humanism, and judicial rectitude. Two: The dark side of the force.'"

Madame Sardikos raised an eyebrow and fingered her rope of pearls, then she picked up the next book on the stack and opened it. "*This* is in Mamnu," she said. "'All material in this volume, classified in any manner whatsoever by the Holy Hu-

132

man Empire, has been authorized for release in Malusia, by my command.'" She looked up. "It's signed by Sir S. Thibalt Karff, Commander, Imperial Malusian Expeditionary Force. Would that be your Mr. Thibalt, do you think?"

"It looks like his signature, Madame." Melina examined a second book. A letter fell from its pages onto the carpeted floor. Melina knelt and picked it up. "It is addressed to you, Madame," she said, offering the letter to her mistress. The old lady shook her head.

"Read it to me, Melina. I left my glasses in the library."

Melina opened the envelope. "It is undated, Madame, and he begins 'Dear Madame Sardikos—'"

"He addresses me as an equal?"

"Yes, Madame."

"That may or may not be presumptuous. Go on."

"'Permit me to thank you for your recent hospitality. Miss Melina served most admirably to guide me around the city of Enkomi, and her kindness and yours are most appreciated.

"'Events beyond Enkomi have forced me to take my leave of it. I regret only that I was unable to take my leave of you.

"'The Great Holders of Malusia have become the enemies of my enemy. The enumeration of detail would be tedious, but Dr. Philodor Joseph Fouché, the Commissioner of the FURDS/POUM Fleet, has been responsible for the death of more of my people than I care to recall. That he is *your* implacable enemy can hardly be news to you by now.

"'The books, in which this letter was enclosed, provide the basis for understanding MST, mechanically simulated telekinesis. Copies of the books were sent to all the Great Holders, as well as an explanation of MST. What, you ask, is this thing? It is the basis for the propulsion and weapons technology of the FURDS/POUM Fleet, and the principal advantage which that fleet has over Malusia's indigenous forces.

"'There may not be time for you to use this understanding, or even to achieve it, but if you do not make the attempt, you will be defeated and conquered—'" Melina hesitated, "'—piecemeal.' But he spelled it with an *ea*, 'peacemeal'—Perhaps he was making a little joke."

"Or perhaps he couldn't spell," the old lady said grimly.

"On today's news, Madame, Commissioner Fouché was reported as saying that he 'has no territorial ambitions in the

Malusian system beyond Naxos.' Perhaps Mr. Thibalt was trying to tell us something."

"Sir Karff, you mean. Go on."

"'There are two things you must know. First, for the Great Holders, MST is slow poison in a golden chalice. It will make the space elevator obsolete. Your civilization, which made the space elevator its keystone, will fall without it. If you choose *not* to embrace MST, you have no hope of resisting the FURDS/POUM Fleet, and your civilization will die violently and at once. Your only hope is to play for time as you work to gain mastery of the MST technology. Afterward, you will change because you must, but perhaps more slowly.'"

Madame Sardikos coughed. "If we survive, there will *be* no changes."

"'Second,'" Melina continued, "'at the time we met, the Imperial Fleet, which I have the honor to serve, was actively considering the conquest of Malusia. I came to Enkomi as a scout for that fleet. Where is it now? Gone. We came here in the first place because we were fleeing from the Rebellion. When the Rebel (FURDS/POUM) Fleet followed hard on our heels, the Imperial Fleet fled again, leaving me here to fight a rear-guard action. Did I approach you under false colors? Yes. However, the technology of single-cell protein which I gave you is well developed. As, I expect, your laboratories told you.

"'What advice can I give you? Fight, of course. For my sake, as well as your own. In a protracted struggle you must succeed. Never give up.

"'It might be helpful to form a committee of Great Holders to order your defense. True, it would constitute a de facto government, but what are your choices? Rigid adherence to doctrinal purity has become a luxury you cannot afford. Of course, some of your fellows—General Delosian comes to mind—may choose to die rather than to change. Good riddance, say I. You, I believe, will change. Good luck, in the prosecution of your war.' He signs himself Sir Thibalt Karff."

"Indeed," Madame Sardikos said at last, smoothing her black dress. "Sir Thibalt has given me a lot to chew on." The door chimes sounded. "See to the door, Melina."

Melina came back with Gregor Naxos and General Delosian.

"Madame," Gregor began, "Madame Sardikos! Naxos may

fall—Naxos *is* falling! We are trying to mount a relief expedition. General Delosian has agreed to lead it. Will you give us the support of Sardikos?"

"Come in and sit down," the old lady said. "Melina, bring in the tea cart and . . . whatever."

"Time, Madame, is of the essence," General Delosian cried urgently. "At this very moment Naxos stands on the verge of surrender!"

"Don't let me detain you, then," she said. "If running around like a decapitated chicken will save Naxos, go to it."

"The Sardikos battleships at Kaloutsa Naval Base, will you send them?" Naxos asked.

"Sit down, Gregor."

"We need those ships! We must have them!"

"Shouting won't get them for you," Madame Sardikos said coldly. "Neither will making a fist. Sit down or get out!"

"Hey, Gregor," Delosian said, "take it easy. The Madame has some questions. She has a right to know."

"What's to ask?" Gregor wiped his bald head with a handkerchief.

"Why *won't* you sit down?"

He grimaced and shook his head. "Jest at my agitation if you will, Madame, but I assure you—"

"Don't bother." Madame Sardikos cut him off. "You're upset. Palpably upset."

Melina rolled in the tea cart, with a silver teapot and a basket of scones covered with a white linen napkin. The jasmine fragrance of the tea mingled with the yeasty aroma of the hot scones.

"Sit down, Gregor." He shook his head. "What's the matter? Are you afraid that sitting down and thinking about what to do will make us a government?"

"Your goddamned furniture is a pain in the ass," he growled.

"We already know what we have to do," Delosian said brusquely, but he took a seat on the divan, and Melina poured him a steaming cup of pale green tea.

"How fortunate you are," the old lady said as she sat on the straight-backed chair beside the divan, from which vantage she could look down on him. "*I* do not, and usually I count myself highly opinionated." Melina poured for her, and Gregor

Naxos, finding himself standing with the servants, sat down on the other side of the general.

"Tell me—whatever happened to the Naxian war ships around Naxos?" Madame Sardikos asked pleasantly.

A long pause drifted into an embarrassed silence.

"Yes?" she prompted at last.

"They were destroyed in a surprise attack," Gregor's tone was sullen.

"My information was that they were ordered to surrender," she said. "I don't doubt they were surprised, but it wasn't because they weren't alert. What happened?"

"We don't know," Delosian admitted at last.

"I see." She sipped her tea. "But it won't happen to the relief fleet, *will* it?"

General Delosian's lean, leathery face set into a mask of determination.

"I, personally, will lead the relief fleet," he said.

"That doesn't answer my question."

"You think I would willingly go to my death?"

"I wouldn't put it past you, General. You might find it easier than thinking."

"Naxos will fall if we don't act."

"It will fall in any event, Gregor. You received a set of books from Sir Thibalt Karff?"

"And a letter." Delosian said. "The man is daft."

"I disagree."

"Oh?" Both men leaned a little forward on the divan.

"The books, in Imperiales, unfortunately, purport to be the key to a thing called MST, which is the key to the enemy's military technology." She picked a scone out of the basket. "Sardikan engineers and scientists will be assigned to work on them. I, in turn, will seek to buy time for them to work." She ate the scone slowly. Neither man said anything. "I will *not* send our ships at Kaloutsa to relieve Naxos. You understand?"

"No." Gregor Naxos sat with his bald head in his hands.

"Think about it. I play for time because I have hope. You and Delosian here"—she took a sip of tea—"hasten to your destruction because you despair."

"You place your hopes on that silly stack of books?" Delosian's voice was incredulous.

"What other hope is there?"

Gregor Naxos stood up. "Come on, General, we're wasting our time here. Let's see if we can do better with Corsikos."

Delosian picked up a scone. "You go ahead, Gregor." He smiled, the muscles of his face barely relaxing. "I'm not ready to give up yet."

Chapter 17.
Rear Guard Action,
Malusiopolis

AT THE EDGE of the university district in Malusiopolis, Bleck-flotos College maintained an off-campus dormitory for graduate students and junior faculty. A graceless building, it was assembled with prefabricated concrete blocks and garnished with a stainless steel fire escape which added a touch of flash to an otherwise lumpige facade. Professor Jules Pargos-Sardikos lived there in a rent-subsidized apartment.

In the middle of the night he woke to hear his bedroom window being opened. This is a dream, he thought, I must be dreaming. Then the small sharp noise of metal on glass convinced him he was awake. Heart pounding, he sat up. "Where do you think you are?" Jules demanded. "Get *out* of here!" He was blinded by a flashlight shining in his face.

"Excuses. Are you the Mr. Professor Jules Par'oz-Sardi-koz?" a heavily accented voice asked.

"This is his bedroom," Jules conceded cautiously as his feet groped for his slippers. "Who the hell are *you*?"

"Captain Hans Detana," was the baffling reply. "You will come with us, please. Get up, please. Get dressed, please." Then, when Jules did not start moving at once, "*Make fast*, please!" Arcziari played the flashlight over the book-filled room until he found the light switch.

"What is this all about?" Jules demanded when the lights came on. What he saw could not have been reassuring. The huge, ugly Arcziari and the wiry, intense Detana both wore the black duty uniforms of the Imperial Secret Police, with a red armband bearing a white disc. Arcziari was holding a long black flashlight that looked as if it could double as a baton and cattle prod. The machine gun slung over his shoulder was less alarming because it seemed less likely to be used.

"This is your the moment," Detana said. "It is time to underraise the steenking government! But you cannot do it in the pajamas, Mr. Professor."

"Oh?" Jules put on his glasses and stood up. "This is a terrible time to try to do *anything*. How can you even *think* about underraising the government when Naxian pork shipments have been cut off?"

"Naxian *everything* is—how you say it—cut off." By then Detana was pacing back and forth. "You do not hear?"

"Nothing," Jules said, putting on his pants. "Since the food riots, there has been a news blackout. No shortages, but the silly fools panicked and started hoarding."

"Excuse, please," Detana said. "Not silly, not fools, also. When we leave Ayios Sostis—oh, maybe three weeks back— Moptown-bound cargo was being forcibly detained. The freighters being used as emergency warehouses. There *will* be shortages."

Jules paused as he put on his shoes and socks. "No..." he said softly. "No. No! That's the way the '83 started! *That's* the way the Great Hunger began! If that's true, Malusiopolis is dead—what's the point of underraising a government if we're going to die of starvation?"

"Shave, please," Detana said. Numbly, Jules went into the bathroom and kicked on his electric razor.

The transporter picked them up from the fire escape and set them down on a platform built on the roof of an empty warehouse on the other side of the city. The platform had an unpainted wooden rail and led to a spiral staircase under a kind of gazebo.

Detana and Professor Jules went down the stainless steel stairs into an empty and dimly lit room containing some unimpressive chemical apparatus. The air smelled of methanol and aromatic organic chemicals.

"Good evening, Professor." Karff stepped into the light. "So kind of you to come!" Sir Karff was wearing Imperial black, but the dress blacks, put together by a local tailor, with the Knight's Cross at the throat. He looked impressive as hell. "Professor, let me introduce you to some of your most ardent supporters. This is George Boulos, the head of the Boulos Group." George was bigger than Arcziari and fat. He had a scar on one side of his face, tattoos on his arms, and he smelled of expensive cologne. They shook hands, and his grip was curiously gentle, as if he didn't want to break anything.

"'Splasher' Perros," Karff continued, "head of the Perros Group." The Splasher was short and pudgy, but his personality was electric. "Mr. Perros has agreed to head up the police for us. Mr. Boulos, the army."

"Hey, Colonel," Perros said, "we'll have the ration books printed up by tomorrow night."

"With the ID card?"

"Yeah. Otherwise we'd have 'em already."

"Ration books?" Jules asked.

"The ships in the pipeline—the ones still en route to Moptown—stop arriving in four weeks," Karff said. "We can feed everybody, but just barely. You understand? If nobody profits, nobody starves." Jules nodded.

He met the head warden from the Kalavassos and his two deputies, and a group of six distinguished prisoners. And businessmen. And contractors. And media people. And assorted academics.

"I believe you already know Dr. Claude Bergeret-Naxos, the president of the university," Karff said.

"I've shaken his hand in a receiving line." Jules appeared to be dazed. "What *is* this, anyway?"

"We are underraising the government," Dr. Bergeret-Naxos said, "and we would like you to head it up."

"Why me?"

"You've talked it up enough. You've gone from lemma to axiom to theory. Now, we hope, to praxis."

"Do you take me for a fool, Thibalt?" Jules glared around him. "I have no guns, no power—why *me*?"

"Heh..." Karff gave a mirthless chuckle. "Because you aren't one of *them*." He gestured with one hand, to include the men Jules had just met. "Aren't you going to ask about the government we'd like you to lead?" Jules nodded.

"The Republic of Malusiopolis," Dr. Bergeret-Naxos announced. "As president, your role will be largely ceremonial, presiding over the opening of a Parliament which we will have to elect, awarding honors, that sort of thing. There had been some thought of making you a king, but there was the problem of your succession—you *are*, after all, a Sardikos—and we decided on a president, instead. A constitution is being drawn up. Your friend Sir Karff is heading the committee. Institutions are being organized. Elections will be held. Malusiopolis is on the move!"

"Well, look," Jules countered, "unless you can feed the people, all this is just a sick joke. And if you can't feed the people, I want no part of *it* or *you*!"

"That's fair, Jules," Karff said. "Gentlemen, may I have your indulgence to go over the pilot plant here one more time? For the benefit of our president-elect." He walked over to a five-thousand-liter holding tank, obviously secondhand. "Methyl alcohol," he said, patting it. "Our basic feedstock. It runs through this yellow pipe. *This*" —he patted a second tank next to it—"is basically hard water with a little phosphate and a few vitamins. It runs through the blue pipe." He walked over to a gray box. "See, the blue pipe and the yellow pipe come into the metering valve here—it has some sensors and chips to keep it running right—and the mixed feed stock runs into the bottom of the reactor." He walked over to the reactor and turned on the light inside. Jules went over and looked through the window. Inside, a murky liquid churned around, throwing a yellowish crud to the surface, and against the walls, where a circular path was cleaned by a slowly rotating scraper which unloaded itself in a hole in the side of the reactor.

"The hole goes to the dryer," Karff said. "Eventually, we'll recycle the recovered methanol, but right now, we don't bother. There isn't that much of it." He walked over to the end of the dryer and opened it. The smell of methanol suddenly was stronger, and inside the dryer box a rotating pipe slowly dribbled a brownish powder into a fiber drum lined with plastic. "Chickens love it," Karff noted. "It's bland, but people can eat it as a sole diet. Especially if it's mixed with a little microcrystalline cellulose for bulk. Can we feed the people? Hell *yes*, we can feed the people!"

Professor Jules reached in and ate some of the brown powder. "This isn't bad, actually," he said. "Can you scale this up? I mean, can we *really* feed ourselves, Karff?"

"No problem. This is a mature technology. Politically, of course, it can't be done without a government."

"Yes. Yes. I see . . ." Professor Jules felt his hastily shaved jaw. "The Great Holders always blocked our attempts to feed ourselves because if we could raise food, we could raise a government. I guess we'll find out if they were right, won't we?" He turned away from the pilot plant and lifted his arms to his audience. "If you want me as your president, I will serve. I am honored beyond my wildest dreams! Long live the Republic of Malusiopolis!"

The audience seemed a little uncertain how to respond. They started to applaud when Karff, standing behind Professor Jules, made a vigorous stand-up gesture with both hands, and as they began to stand . . .

"Long live the Republic!!" Karff shouted.

That did it. Whatever they might have thought privately, it was good participatory theater, and they stood up shouting, "Long live the Republic!" and "Long live the president!" The old warehouse echoed and reechoed with cries of "Long live!" for several minutes.

When the initial enthusiasm had subsided, Karff led Jules over to the chief warden. "We have several gentlemen here from the Kalavassos," Karff noted politely. "May I suggest that for your first official act, you pardon them?" The gentlemen in question, Great Holders that it was inconvenient to have on the outside, were standing beside the warden.

President Jules looked them over. "We don't want to be *too* merciful."

"Heaven forbid." Karff somehow managed to keep his face perfectly straight. "However, none of them are *your* enemies."

"You think it's all right?" Then, taking a deep breath, the president decided. "Hah! I'll *do* it! What do I do?"

"I have the papers right here," the Chief Warden said. "All you have to do is sign them."

Chapter 18.
Moptown Politics

THE OFFICE MIGHT not have been larger than a football field, but it wasn't much smaller than a basketball court. One of the Great Holders had operated his business interests in Malusiopolis in that very room.

"These are in production now." Karff pushed a little black box across his enormous conference desk to Splasher Perros. "Push the red button."

Perros pushed the button, and the box unfolded with a gentle click to reveal a small platen and a liquid crystal display.

"Put your thumb on the platen."

Perros did so, and the digital version of his thumbprint appeared on the display screen, together with the date and time. "Hey, great!" Perros said, "we can verify ID on the spot!"

"You can check it, too," Karff added. "The patrol skimmer has an index list of all the prints on file, right? Read off the numbers, it tells you who you have—or maybe more important, that you have somebody we never heard of. Somebody we maybe ought to look into."

"Son of a bitch! This mother is in production?"

"Watch your fucking language. President Jules is a bit of a prude."

"Right, Karff, right . . ." Perros agreed, grinning. "We don't want to upset the little fella. You said this was in production?"

"Yes. They told me they were running off ninety to a hundred a day on three shifts. A few weeks, every cop on the beat will have one."

"Hey, Colonel, we got more cops than *that*."

"So, production figures to pick up. Take it. Use it in good health."

"I will," Perros agreed. "Hey, I've got to run."

The next visitor was Sergeant Stavo. "My God, Colonel! You could park the transporter in here . . ."

"Not quite," Karff replied pleasantly. "What's going on over at the Bleckflotos Secret Weapons Works?"

"Hmm—the MST library I had has finally been translated and put in hard copy. I had no idea how *big* it was, you know?" He sat down at Karff's invitation. "The thing is, we have a whole lot of really bright guys, you know?"

"We'd *better* have."

"Right. Look, Colonel—you know the Gaussian distribution curve?" Karff nodded. "Well, the curve for the guys who try for an advanced degree in MST, I've got to be pretty far down on the dumb end. You know what I mean? These guys—these guys are *sharp*, sir. They are way the hell over on the sharp end of the curve. I mean, they are *smart*."

"I should hope so. We told the university that MST had a top-priority rating. Are they giving you a hard time?"

"Oh, no, sir. Nothing like that. See, the first couple of weeks were pretty good. I was the old head. I was teaching 'em the basics, the stuff I had down real good. The second couple of weeks I was hanging in there, but they were cutting the stuff it had taken years to pound into my thick head like it was *easy*, you know? But I was hanging in there. And I could tell them where to look or what questions to ask, sometimes." Stavo sat back in his chair and rested his hands on the arms. "Now I'm out of it. I come in, and they're jabbering in Mamnu, and I can't understand. Only, one of them will come around and translate for me, and I *still* can't understand. I can't understand the MST."

"You don't want to be an administrator? You know the people. You just keep things running smoothly. You don't have to do the work yourself, Sergeant."

"No, sir. When I was a recruit, I was out on detail with another fella, shoveling sand onto a sieve, and we had a corporal along. And he supervised for about ten minutes, and then he grabbed the extra shovel and pitched in. I suppose he was bored. But I'm more like him than I am like some clown who stands around watching the work being done. Begging your pardon, sir."

"No offense, Stavo. You want to go back to the transporter?"

"Yes, sir."

"Very well. As soon as we can find a replacement for you. You aren't doing a bad job at all over there, you know, just staying out of the way of the people doing the work." Karff rubbed his eyes. "Would you like a degree? I could ask the Dean of Bleckflotos College to award you an honorary degree as a thank you for the work you put in—" The phone rang, and he picked it up.

"The skimmer is here to take you to the ceremony," his secretary announced. "You *are* running a bit behind, sir."

"I'll be right down." Karff stood up and turned to Stavo. "*That* was a nice piece of work," he said. "The main single-cell protein factory going on line less than two weeks after the last grain ship arrived. Do you want an honorary degree, Stavo?"

"I don't know, sir. I don't really feel I earned it, if you know what I mean."

"I understand," said Karff. He leaned over his desk and wrote 'Stavo off TDY ASAP.' "But it will make *them* feel better about it."

The skimmer was long and black and glossy, with the exposed engine part finished in bright chrome. Two police skimmers were positioned fore and aft, the heart and swords of the Perros Group overlaid with the decal of the Republic, a red circle on a white field, the circle enclosing the outline of a blue three-pointed star, superimposed over a solid blue three-pointed star. Underneath, it said M.P.D. CAR 441, on the aft skimmer.

They roared off and arrived at the SCP Plant precisely at the appointed hour. A crowd of thousands had gathered, and a band was playing. Boulosi patrolled. They had short machine guns and wore red, white, and blue arm bands in lieu of uniforms. Karff noted that the army used a white disc on a red field, while the police used a red circle on a white field. Different shades of blue, too.

Then he was on the platform with President Jules Pargos-Sardikos, and his newly acquired group of hangers-on. The dedication went flawlessly.

At the reception afterward, Jules and his entourage, a bodyguard, a secretary, a strikingly beautiful blonde of no discernible function, two lawyers, and his cousin, Peter Cretos-Pargos, gathered around Karff at the side of the room.

145

"We have looked over the draft of the proposed constitution," Jules said. "Frankly, Mr. Thibalt, I must tell you that it is less than totally acceptable."

"My cousin puts it very gently, indeed." Peter was leaning on his silver-headed cane. "Except for a few sentences scattered throughout the body of the draft, it is totally *un*acceptable." He reached in his pocket and removed a heavily marked-up copy of the draft. "Do you understand?"

Karff took a sip of champagne and smiled. "You don't like it."

"Don't play the smartass. This is serious!"

"Forgive me. I defer to your greater sense of self-importance."

"Now look—" Peter began, starting to raise his cane.

"Gently, cousin." Jules put his hand on the cane arm. "He didn't mean to insult you."

"Certainly not," Karff agreed. "In that case you would have been properly insulted. May I see the mark-up of the draft, please?"

Peter handed it to him. "Keep it. That's a copy."

"Actually," one of the lawyers added, "this is rather more what we had in mind. The role you seem to have in mind for the president is . . . is . . ."

"Ridiculous," the other lawyer said.

"I'm sure *Sir* Karff will be happy to do it our way, won't you, Sir Karff?" Peter said. The emphasis on the title underlined the fact that Karff was an outsider, not a citizen of Malusiopolis.

"Perhaps," Karff said smoothly, as he looked over the mark-up. "You have a highly unrealistic idea of what you can accomplish in the real world. Do you think that George Boulos will let you appoint anybody you like to head up the army, which is, after all, mostly the Boulos Group? Or that Splasher Perros will let you take the police away from him?"

"If it is the will of the people," Peter said.

"And if the people want what you don't?"

"They will be reeducated!"

Karff browsed through the marked-up copy of the draft, sipping his champagne, and finally put it in his pocket.

"This *could* be put in," he said at last.

Jules grinned. "Good. Excellent! I knew you'd see it our way!"

"However..." There was a pregnant silence. Karff looked up apologetically. "I'm afraid that once this actually is in place, there is no *way* you are going to continue to hold office, Mr. President."

"He *is* president," Peter stated. "And he is, by God, going to *stay* president! That is a *fact*!"

Karff replaced his empty glass on a passing tray and picked up a fresh one.

"You are ill-advised by this gimpy fool, Mr. President," he said. "Put—"

"Gimpy!?" Peter turned bright red and raised his cane to start a blow. Karff threw champagne in his face and took the cane away from him.

"Gimpy," Karff repeated. Peter clenched his teeth and clutched the fingers of the hand that had held the cane. "Don't utter a threat you can't enforce." He turned to Jules. "As for you, Mr. President—I'd seek other counsel if I were you."

"Dirty bastard!" Peter snarled.

"A word of advice, Mr. Cretos-Pargos." Karff pointed the head of the cane at his belt buckle. "At this range, use your cane to thrust." He pushed the cane forward a little for emphasis. "And keep it low." He reversed the cane and handed it over. Peter took it with his good hand. "A second word of advice: Try it again, I'll break you in half."

"You've made a bad enemy," the second lawyer said.

"Now see here, Mr. Thibalt, I am the president, after all, and under this ludicrous document the president is totally devoid of any power, real or imaginary."

"That's the whole idea. That's why *you* were picked for the slot."

"What do you mean?"

"You're an intellectual, Mr. President. Intellectuals aren't *supposed* to have power."

Chapter 19.

Revision of Pattern for Conquest, II

ON THE *Grendlsmöder*, the flagship of the FURDS/POUM Fleet, sitting 220 kilometers off Naxos, Commissioner P. Joseph Fouché lit one long, scented cigarette with the butt of another.

"Taking this filthy rat-hole has proved to be unacceptably costly," he said bitterly. "We have no reinforcements, and no prospects of reinforcements. We are on our own! Do you understand?"

"You demanded a victory, regardless of cost," the bald admiral reminded. "You have it. Don't complain to *me* about casualties!"

Fouché took a long drag on his cigarette and stubbed it out. "The Great Holders were supposed to collapse. Instead the fools chatter inanely about us going home. We have shed too much blood to go home! We can only go forward! We *are* committed—we *must* conquer this place. But not with the marines. Not with brute force." He shook his head. "And for God's sake, no more corridor-to-corridor, room-to-room fighting in a strange habitat. We must use finesse. Does *no* one here understand strategic thinking?!"

"By an amazing coincidence, sir," the one-eyed admiral replied, "it just happens that I have a proposal—"

"You aren't trying to replay the Lyonsk campaign, are you?"

"Oh, no, sir." The one-eyed admiral wore the faintest of smiles. "As you, yourself, very astutely pointed out, Lyonsk was Lyonsk, and Malusia is Malusia. What I propose to do is use our naval superiority to establish a blockade of Enkomi and the space elevator. We intercept the light-sail cargo ships—which are robot-controlled—with long-range tractor beams.

This will impose no costs on us, and severely disrupt the Malusian economy."

"Will it, indeed?"

"Yes, Joseph," the Deputy Commissioner said. "The cities of Malusia are totally dependent on the shipment of food from the habitats."

"Hey, Padre—we want to conquer the *habitats*! Starving a third party won't do it for us. Besides, they'll let the cities starve and blame *us* for it, and that will psych them up to fight even harder."

"We could divert the cargo to Malusia, sir," the third admiral said.

"Oh?" Fouché looked interested. "How would you do that?"

"No problem, sir. We use a space station and a ground station. The *Ancalagon* for the space station, the *Glaurung* for the ground station. There is no way we can take the *Glaurung* back through *i*-space—"

"So it is expendable," Fouché said, lighting a cigarette. "Yes. So we divert the flow of cargo from the space elevator. Then what?"

"The Malusian cities fall to us, or they don't get fed," the Deputy Commissioner said. "If the Great Holders stop sending food, the cities will starve, and *they* will feel guilty about it. In the circumstances, I would expect them to come to terms."

The Commissioner exhaled smoke and nodded. "Yes. Yes, that might work. Where would we put the ground station?"

"The logical site just happens to be Malusiopolis, sir," said the one-eyed admiral with a poker face. "However, I am sure that there are other sites that will serve nearly as well."

The bald admiral opened a file folder. "Malusiopolis is in a state of rebellion against the Great Holders. Perhaps as a result of our action at Naxos. If so, they might welcome us as allies and liberators."

"Ye-es..." Fouché held the cigarette in nicotine-stained fingers as ash spilled on the map. "They might not, also. I don't like trying to put down a ground station in contested territory."

"Of *course*, Joseph—you can't even *run* a ground station in contested territory. We taught the Empire that; *we* aren't going to forget it. On the other hand, there may not be a contest."

"And if there were," the third admiral said, "the Malusians don't have MST, so they couldn't really make a fight of it. If you know what I mean, sir."

"Yes." Fouché scowled. "At least scout the place before you go charging in. Send Max Pavakian and some of his Naxian turncoats. To Malusiopolis."

Chapter 20.

The War Comes to Malusiopolis

IT WAS A cold, gray day with flurries of snow gusting on the north wind, as Karff's skimmer pulled up in front of army headquarters. An aide brought him to General Boulos, who escorted him into the basement.

"They say, you know, they say that when you splashed the drink into that banker's fat face, it was because he wouldn't come to bed with you," Boulos said in his gravelly bass. "Is that true?"

"Eh?" Karff looked up at the big man. "No. Who is the 'they' that said such horseshit?"

"The President's Party—maybe not Jules himself—but people close to him." Boulos shrugged. "You were there. Who saw it?"

"Jules. His gimpy cousin. Hangers-on. Who put out the story?"

"I'll have someone check it out," the big man replied. "The reason I ask 'is it true' is that I don't want you to do it here. There might be shooting. You understand, personally I don't give a shit, but some of my boys...you could give them offense very easily, like that."

"You give *me* offense," Karff said. "The offense that someone in high position could be so painfully dumb."

Boulos grinned, showing a chipped tooth. "You'll get used to it. Here we are."

'Here' was a temporary detention center, a cafeteria opening onto an atrium filled with cots and prisoners, who were sitting around. They walked to the back of the cafeteria, and sat down at a round yellow table while the guards hustled to bring the prisoners.

"How come the army made the arrest?" Karff asked.

"Hee hee . . ." giggled Boulos. "There was a jurisdictional dispute, you might say. Luckily we didn't lose any of the prisoners."

Five men and a woman were led in, all somewhat the worse for wear. One of the men had his right arm in a sling. He looked up at Karff, and there was a mutual shock of recognition.

"And I had just got done saying nothing else could go wrong," he said. "Good afternoon, Colonel Karff."

"Hello, Pavakian."

"You know this fellow?" Boulos asked.

"Max Pavakian, aka Dr. Fang, aka SMASHER ONE." Karff nodded. "If he were my prisoner, I'd shoot him out of hand."

"Really? On what charges?"

"Terrorism. Murder. Torture. None of them in your jurisdiction, so far as I know. He *is* from the FURDS/POUM Fleet."

"Ah." Boulos nodded and rubbed his chin. "And the others are Naxians?"

Karff leaned forward on the table. "What about it, Pavakian?"

"What about what, Colonel?"

"Your companions. Where are they from?"

"The lower classes of Naxos. They are here to strike a blow for human freedom and human liberty."

"Lower classes?" Karff smiled faintly. "They look like a pack of failed librarians—intellectual jackals following a real tiger." He turned to Boulos. "Find out in detail who his companions are. What his orders were. How he got here. When he was due to return. I'd like to know why he was sent, but he probably doesn't know. You've made an important catch. Do you want any help with the interrogation?"

"No, no." Boulos shook his massive head. "We just go at him in relays for a few days and grind the bastard down. You've given us all the handle we need."

Outside, as Karff's sleek black skimmer with the chrome-plated tripartite manifold pulled away from the dock in front of the building, he went into the tiny cabin and called the transporter.

Ildenhagen answered. "Look," said Karff, "we've picked up a fellow from the FURDS/POUM Fleet. How did he get here, do you think?"

"Via transporter," Ildenhagen said. "In which case, it could be hanging around to take him home."

"That's pretty much what I thought. Can you spot the mother?"

"Maybe. If we get lucky. What we'll do is break out of the clouds where *we* have been keeping the proverbial low profile and put the blue and green filters on the telescopic cameras. Then we check topside visually for the son of a bitch." The luminous bottom of the transporter did not exactly match the spectra of the luminous sky. With the blue and green filters in place, the sky appeared a very dark red, and the transporter a bright red. "If he isn't upstairs, then *we* go upstairs and try looking down. If he ever comes out of the clouds, we'll spot him. Otherwise..." she sighed. "You want a call when we luck out?"

Karff was in his office working on a coordinated revision of the proposed constitution when Ildenhagen called him back.

"We have him, sir," Ildenhagen said. "Altitude, 10,500 meters, vector 172. Orders?"

"Hold your fire and get back under cover. I'm going to see if the locals can take him out." Karff pulled at his nose. "I'll call the airport. Wait. What's the vector from the *airport*?"

"From there?" Ildenhagen paused a second. "Vector 249.5... call it 250. Almost due east. The range—do you want the range?"

"Yes. That's the range from the airport, right?"

"Yes, sir. Range is 45.2 kilometers."

"Target motion?"

"We haven't been watching long enough to be sure. It appears to be holding."

"Good. From the airport, then, vector 250, range 45.2 kilometers, altitude 10,500 meters. I'll see if I can get some action on it."

He dialed the airport.

"Airport information service. This is a recording. Please stand by. All our lines are temporarily busy." He hung up the phone in disgust. Who was over there? He walked to the north window in his office and looked over at the airport, dirty white and metallic gray in the late afternoon sunlight. He could *see* military jets sitting on the runway. They were—he searched through his memory—the Zouave Secret Squadron or something equally stupid. He looked in the phone book under "Zouave" and found nothing.

He put away the phone book and called his secretary. "I want to talk to airport security," he said. Five minutes later he was talking to a very young lieutenant who was holding down the post.

"You have some military jets out there. Can you put me through to their leader?"

"Jets, Colonel?" The tone of voice betrayed total incomprehension.

"Warplanes, Lieutenant," Karff said gently. "The Republic of Malusiopolis kind of inherited them from Naxos or someplace. Can you put me through to their leader?"

"Oh. That would be on the military side of the airport. They have their own security setup, Colonel, sir. I'll transfer you—"

"Give me the number first," Karff said very quickly.

"Yes, sir. The number is 123-4876."

The call was transferred, and Karff found himself talking to someone with a bad connection. He hung up and called the number.

"Czouave Security, Sergeant Moakely speaking."

"Good. This is Colonel Karff. Can you put me through to the commander of the squadron?"

"You mean Air Marshal Czouavos? He's gone home for the day."

"I see. Is no one there authorized to take those jets up in his absence?"

"Yes, sir." There was a long pause. "No one can take them up without his say-so, sir."

"We hope emergencies are so kind as to come during working hours. Can you give me the air marshal's home phone, please?"

"No, sir. He went home, and he has an unlisted number."

"I understand. Give me his number, Sergeant."

"I don't have it, sir. He *will* be in tomorrow about nine, if you want to call then. At 123-4500."

"Sergeant, surely Air Marshal Czouavos did *not* simply vanish. Where can I reach him?"

"You *can't*, Colonel."

Karff pulled his nose between thumb and forefinger. "I understand. Are there any *pilots* standing by?"

"Yes, sir—but they aren't let fly without the air marshal's orders."

"May I talk to them?"

"No, sir, they're on duty." There was a long, long pause. "Is there some sort of emergency, sir?"

"I am going to come over there *personally*," Karff said. "If you can think of any way to get to the air marshal, it would probably be in your best interest to do so."

It took ten minutes to round up a platoon of effectives, Perrosi KP's from the mess hall and assorted troublemakers confined to the barracks. They slipped on their white armbands—'The blue star of hope, surrounded by red tape, lost in the fog of confusion'—and their short machine guns, and went racing over to the airport in three skimmers, including Karff's own.

They slid through the gate on the civilian side of the airport and drove directly across the field to the warplanes, two groups of four each sitting in the spacious hangar, and a third group of four out on the tarmac.

Karff sent his Perrosi commandos out into the hangar, where they secured the planes and set up a perimeter, capturing and disarming a single guard in the process. Karff picked up the phone and dialled 123-4876.

"Czouave Security. Sergeant Moakely speaking."

"This is Colonel Karff, Sergeant. I stopped by the hangar with some of my people, and we seem to have captured all your bloody warplanes!"

"Colonel Karff, sir—*what*?"

We captured your airplanes. Did you get in touch with the air marshal?"

"Ah . . . no, sir. How did you get through the gate?"

"What gate?"

"The main military gate. They weren't supposed to let you in."

"Hey, Sergeant—will you tell the pilots to fall in over here? I want to talk to them."

"What do you want to talk to *them* for, sir?"

"I want to tell them how bloody awful their security is, you

155

fool! And if you don't get them over *immediately*, I'll *do* it! Now will you get them *out* here?!"

A dozen pilots showed up, wearing gray coveralls and carrying red crash helmets marked with a golden crescent. As a concession to the Republic of Malusia, they had sewn on a little patch of red tape with an embroidered white circle and blue star over the left jacket pocket.

Karff walked out on the front of his skimmer. "All right, men. An airship of the FURDS/POUM Fleet is hanging around our fair Republic. A transporter. You've seen what they look like. Some of you have clipboards. A couple of minutes ago it was at vector 252, altitude 10,300 meters, range 45.8 kilometers. You have it? The son of a bitch is hovering up there for no good purpose. Now, goddamn it, I want you to go up there and shoot the bastard down!"

"I know you, sir," one of the pilots said. "You brought in the plans for the food factory, and that was a good piece of work, but we don't take *your* orders, sir."

"Are you the senior officer here?"

"*I'm* the senior officer," a stocky, bald man announced, "Major Harros."

"Very good, Major Harros. The enemy is up there in a transporter. Will you go up and attack them?"

"They are *your* enemy, sir. They may not be *our* enemy."

"Hey, the Republic of Malusiopolis is a sovereign state, right? So if those bastards were friendly, they'd land at the airport. We found out they were up there after we caught some spies and terrorists they landed in Malusiopolis *itself*. In *your* territory, Major. Now, tell me, how can they not be enemy?"

"They might just be looking us over, sir."

"Naxos fell last week, and now they're looking at *us*, and that doesn't bother you, Major Harros? It is your sworn duty to defend Moptown against its enemies, Major. Now, will you go up and shoot them the hell down?"

"Not without orders from the air marshal, sir."

"Where *is* the air marshal?" another pilot asked.

"At home with his unlisted number," Karff answered. "Where's your goddamned *mothers*? Ask *them* for permission to take off!"

He stepped down into the skimmer's cockpit. "My apologies. I thought you people were *fighters*. Strike group! Return to your craft! *Make fast!*" His platoon began trotting back to skimmers.

"Wait a minute..." Harros said.

"Goodnight, ladies," Karff called as the last of his troopers climbed back on board. Then the three skimmers went scooting across the airfield into the setting sun.

They were slowing up to pass out through the civilian gate when the thunder of the first four jets taking off reached them. Karff called Ildenhagen.

"Hey, we have some action," he said.

"It *took* you long enough," Ildenhagen said.

"Right. Stick your nose up through the clouds and see if you can give the air force a hand, will you?"

The first flight of four jets broke through the roof of clouds as the second group of four was rolling down the runway.

Climbing to 13,000 meters, they turned to vector 300, hoping, perhaps, to mislead the FURDS/POUM transporter by not coming directly at it. The radar man wasn't fooled, and neither was the FAD operator. The FAD-200, although relatively weak, and subject to being overpowered in a FAD-active environment, was still a versatile instrument. The FAD operator on the Rebel transporter set his axe on the hit mode and loaded it with a retroreflective marker disc, the standard disc, 200 millimeters in diameter, 100 grams in mass, and started tracking the lead plane with the main laser.

When the planes banked and turned, at a range of only 2,700 meters, he depressed the firing button. The lead plane exploded, and the FAD operator slid another marker disc into the breach. The three remaining planes sprayed the airship with cannon fire, seagulls peppering a whale with firecrackers.

On the Imperial transporter in the evening shadows far below, Sergeant Stavo looked up.

"We have a fix on the Rebel FAD," he said.

"Hit 'em," Ildenhagen commanded.

Stavo pressed the firing button, and his 100-gram target was accelerated with a force of 200 joules over a range of 53.2 kilometers. After an elapsed time of 243 milliseconds, the target hit the enemy FAD with a terminal velocity of 1.65 million kilometers per hour. In a vacuum, the speed would have been

157

even higher, since about 10 percent of the available energy had been used to overcome air resistance. No matter how you figure it, a sharp blow.

The Rebel transporter heeled over, and powdered magnesium, mixed with magnesium hydride, began spilling into the evening air, burning with a sprightly incandescence, like sparklers at a lawn party. Then, as the three remaining jets turned around to make a second pass, a line of pale blue flame appeared along the forward hull, and the burning transporter fell out of control.

Captain Ildenhagen turned away in horror from the display screen and picked up the phone.

"He's down, Colonel," she said quietly.

Chapter 21.
Karff Strikes Back

To prosecute the war, the Enkomi Chamber of Commerce formed itself into a committee of the whole. And because that was such an obviously unwieldy and cumbersome method of doing business, a steering committee was designated.

The Committee for the Prosecution, as it was called, consisted of nine members, four of whom could constitute a quorum if the chairman, General Delosian, and the secretary, Madame Sardikos, were present. They met in the Blue Conference Room, a small chamber that had lately been used for storage. It had a white ceiling, pale blue walls, and a dark blue carpet, shot with red and gold swirls. A very ordinary conference table was surrounded with unmatched wooden chairs, and along one wall were lined another six or seven chairs.

"That brings us to new business," Delosian remarked, looking quite dapper in his army uniform. "Tony?"

"Colonel Tony, if you don't mind, sir," said Colonel Antony Melos, the second son of Petrus Melos. "I move that we recognize the Republic of Malusiopolis."

"Second," said Madame Cretos-Pargos, a lean and wrinkled dowager with cool blue eyes. She wore a massive turquoise and silver necklace, with ensemble belt and bracelet.

"We have a motion and a second," Delosian said. "Is there any discussion?"

"Malusiopolis may not be of one mind about this," Madame Sardikos said. "The president has written to urge that we withhold recognition until the local constitution is amended to give him the power that is rightfully his."

"We *do* have to look out for our relatives," Madame Cretos-Pargos noted, "and President Jules Pargos-Sardikos is indeed my darlin' cousin, but we *also* have to ask how it will affect the war. I personally think that Julie is being a little pig-headed here."

"Besides which, we have reports that the FURDS/POUM Fleet has started to move against Malusiopolis," Melos said. "As of oh-three-hundred hours this morning, major units of the fleet were forming up over Malusiopolis at an altitude of about twenty thousand kilometers."

"What major units?" Madame Sardikos asked.

"The *Ancalagon* for one, the *Glaurung* for another."

"I understood that the *Glaurung* had been disabled," Delosian said, "that it couldn't move under its own power."

"That may be true," Melos agreed, "but it remains a formidable weapons platform. We ought to encourage Malusiopolis to fight."

"Whatever for?" Madame Sardikos asked. "How will Malusiopolis be in any *way* decisive in this conflict? How *can* it be?"

"Rather easily." George Corsikos looked over his rimless glasses. "If the FURDS/POUM Fleet takes Malusiopolis, what will they do with it? All it is is a harbor at the end of the line, right? But it *is* a harbor. And if the FURDS/POUM people take it, they have access to the planet of Malusia. *And* superiority in space. For at least a year. What would they do? If I were they, I would divert our shipments of cargo from the space elevator to the ground and space station they will undoubtedly set up at Malusiopolis. And offer to feed the Malusian cities— even Ayios Sostis—from the other end of the existing supply line. At which time, we have lost the war. What is Enkomi without commerce flowing through it? And without Enkomi, how will you hold the habitats? They will fall all over themselves to make a separate peace, to salvage a few crumbs from defeat."

"We *ought* to encourage Malusiopolis to fight," Madame Sardikos agreed. "*I* don't have any objections to my nephew Julie's remaining a figurehead. It rather suits him, actually."

"All in favor of recognizing the Republic of Malusiopolis, signify by saying aye," General Delosian called. "It appears to be unanimous."

"With one abstention," Madame Sardikos said.

"Note it in the minutes," he agreed.

* * *

Feyodor Perros, formerly the Splasher, dapper in a white silk suit with a red brocade vest, walked across Karff's office with a kind of insouciant strut. "Nice little place you have here, Thibalt," he said genially. "You heard I dissolved the Perros Group?"

Karff sat back in his tall leather chair. "I heard you put the whole lot on the public payroll as the Moptown State Police."

"Well, we can't just turn the boys out to fend for themselves. The thing is, I'm running for Parliament, and I don't want it to look like I'm trying to take over. It's the Constitutional Party, not the Perrosi Party, you know what I mean?" He grinned. "I'm going to be the next premier—the *first* premier, actually; we haven't had one yet. But I need good people on the ticket. People I can trust, you know? Who also have to be elected."

"Good luck."

"So I'm scratching around for names. Do you know how many people forty-three is? I mean, when you have all these qualifications you have to put on. I'd like you to stand for Parliament on the Constitutional Party ticket."

"Thanks, but no thanks. I helped you people write the thing, but I will not run for Parliament."

"Hey, Thibalt..." Perros pulled up a straight chair to his desk, and sat with his arms resting on the back. "Why not? You're a shoo-in. You're an authentic hero, for God's sake! You've got great name-recognition, you're even a good speaker. Besides, I need your help! You've *got* to run!"

"No. In the old days, back at the police academy, one of the things they taught us was that your training shaped you physically. You go for a career in security, it shapes you, and there are things you can do and other things that you can't. Running for public office is one of the things that you can't do. The electorate looks at you, and they see a very mean man. And if you put on a kind face, they see a liar."

"That's bunk," Perros said. "Everybody running for office is going to be lying in their teeth the whole total time. You, at least they know a little."

"The other thing," Karff said patiently, "is the matter of loyalty. I made my bones in the service of the Holy Human Empire. You say I've done a lot for Malusiopolis, and it's true, but it just happened that *your* interests and the Empire's interests

161

were running parallel. Do you think I give a shit about your two-bit Republic or your grubby politics? No! What I did was done in the service of the Holy Human Empire! And if they ever come back, my loyalty is with *them* and not with *you*. And, no, I'm not going to stand for election in your silly Parliament."

"Right. *You*, by God, are Sir Thibalt Karff, and running for office in a dump like Moptown is beneath your dignity. Well, I'm telling you, the work you began isn't finished yet." He folded his hands and leaned forward a little for emphasis. "And the Empire, your Holy Human Empire, it isn't coming back. Not now. Not next year. Not *ever*. You aren't a young man, Thibalt. You ought to be thinking about making some money."

For a second Karff had a vivid mental image of a floor littered with Reichsbank Imperiales, and Judge Saloman Azzaro hanging above. Perros is right, he thought sadly, the Empire isn't coming back. And I have to make a living. Somehow. "Perhaps I should," he said at last.

"You do that." Perros nodded his head. "I still want your support."

"You have it."

"And I still need someone to fill out the slot on the ticket. If not you, what about someone in your group?"

Karff pondered the matter for a few moments. "There's Judith," he said at last. "She's the only one in the whole crew who can speak Mamnuish well enough to campaign in it."

"Judith? Judith who? Do I know her?"

"Judith Rakoczy, she's the one I put in at the Bleckflotos Secret Weapons Works when Stavo resigned. As acting administrator."

"I know her." Perros looked thoughtful. "She might do. She just might. Does she take orders?"

Karff laughed. "More or less. More when she feels like it. She keeps her word. If she says she'll do something, if you can *get* her to say she'll do something, you can depend on it."

"Very interesting." Feyodor Perros stood up and walked slowly over to the window looking over the airport. "We could use a woman on the ticket," he said at last. "Do you think she could be elected?"

"I don't know," Karff replied, "but I'll campaign for her."

* * *

Judith looked out of the television set, wearing a severely tailored suit of charcoal-gray sharkskin and a high-necked blouse.

"Good evening, Ladies and Gentlemen, Citizens of the Republic. My name is Judith Rakoczy, and I'm standing for one of the at-large seats in Parliament."

Nick Nickolai, third-string anchorman for the Moptown *Star* TV News, sat across the table from Karff with a stein of beer in front of him. Across the room, the camera was set up on its tripod, and the lights, carefully positioned, were turned off.

Nick took a swig of beer and set the stein down. "She's doing better than I ever figured she could. Shit—she might even get elected."

Karff, in his dress blacks with the Knight's Cross at his throat, picked up his coffee cup in one black-gloved hand and refilled it from the thermos. "Of course. That's why I agreed to do this interview."

"Well *su-ure*!" Nick said. "I mean, *shit*! I mean, she might make it *any*way! Did you hear her on the debate last night?"

Karff shook his head. "I've been busy."

"Right." Nick laughed. "Some of us don't *give* a shit about elections, you crafty bastard! She tore into Peter Corsikos-Pargos—"

"*Cretos*-Pargos," Karff corrected.

"The gimp banker," Nick agreed. "When she got done, it rained pieces of banker for three days! I *loved* it! She has one hell of a temper!"

"She has a temper," Karff agreed, "but I don't think she lost it. She also has a tongue like a razor. How is she doing in the polls?"

"She's come up to within two points. If the election was Wednesday instead of tomorrow, she'd take it for sure. Look— she can really use your help. How come you're doing a broadcast interview instead of being up on the platform with her?"

Karff took a sip of coffee. "Because I have to be here."

"Shit, Colonel—*here* is your goddamned bedroom! Are you mad at her or something?"

"Don't act dumber than God made you, Nick," Karff said coldly. "Here is Transporter *42210*, and *here* is about 200 meters above Sithos Point. Which is, in turn, 57.6 kilometers from Malusiopolis, vector 372. That's southeast more or less.

The reason we're in my bedroom is so that we don't get in the way."

"I wouldn't have got in the way," Nick protested.

"You *are* on a warship in a war. Besides, you aren't the only one. *I'm* the Supreme Commander of Imperial Forces on Malusia or something like that. And *I'm* sitting back here so I can let my people do the goddamned job. Without picking on them. All right?"

Nick took a sip of beer. "*What* job?"

"We're going to ambush the *Glaurung*. A 1.1 million ton battlecruiser."

"WHAT?"

"An ambush. The poor bastards haven't got a chance."

The phone rang.

"Ildenhagen here. The *Glaurung* just dropped past twenty-five hundred meters. We're tracking her on the FAD."

"What about radar?" Karff asked.

"The Moptown airport radar was knocked out about an hour ago. We aren't using ours to avoid detection."

"Right. How is the *Glaurung* finding her way down?"

"They're using a ranging laser, Colonel. You can see the red glare reflecting off the rock."

"Carry on, Captain."

"What in bloody hell is happening?" Nick asked, looking alarmed.

"The war." Karff took a sip of coffee. "This table—did you ever take a close look at it? Under the glass top, the carving is the crest of the 164th Infantry Regiment. It doesn't say what planet, and I never found out, but one morning, about seventy years ago, the 164th went out, and they never came back. What happened? I don't know for sure, but about then somebody invented the resonance-paired distractor, and most likely *that* was what got them."

"A new weapon?"

"A device, Nick. It made the Rebellion possible. See, the way it worked"—Karff folded his hands and leaned one arm on the table—"the way it worked was that the Empire went in and out of gravity wells with ground stations and space stations. *Big* FADs, not like the little baby we have on board. Push, pull, click, click, into orbit that quick. The RPD—the reso-nance-paired distractor—well, see, for the big FADs to work, they have to maintain their concentration. And the RPD *distracts* them, like when you suck a lemon at a trumpeter about to hit a high note. So that the big FAD drops what it was trying to lift.

"And the RPD didn't have to be all that close either. A few kilometers. So what it did, was close down the ground stations."

"Couldn't you move the stuff from the *space* stations?" asked Nick.

"Theoretically, yes... A lot of work was done on that, but they never got it operational. The transporters—what we're riding in—were an interim solution. The space station drops them into the upper atmosphere, and they go wherever to deliver. And go back upstairs for pickup off planet. The—"

The phone rang.

"Ildenhagen here. The *Glaurung* is at five hundred meters, descending at four point-five per second. Shall we take them?"

"A little later," Karff said. "We want to minimize countermeasures. Say, when they break cloud cover?"

"Ceiling is one hundred ninety meters," Ildenhagen said. "That will do, Colonel. That will do nicely, thank you."

Karff walked over to the window. "There's the point," he said quietly. "Can you see the laser glow?"

Nick looked out and shook his head. On the scraped flat rocks of Sithos Point, the red line of the Rebel ranging laser was barely visible in the night air, and where it hit, there was hardly more glow than from a small campfire. Once the red line caught your eye, however, it was unmistakable.

The transporter was sitting at the bottom of a rather skimpy cloud layer which was transmitting the pale light of the crescent Aqua Pura. The rocks, mostly granite, shone a dim gray. The bog surrounding them was black, with here and there a ripple of reflected light on the still swamp waters. Around the edge of the point, mangroves grew in dark profusion, textured black upon the black bog. The eye came back to the red line of the ranging laser.

"I see it," Nick announced at last. "Where did you get this distractor thing?"

"We used the hardware of the FAD-200. And the MST task force over at Bleckflotos College programmed the resonance-paired distractor right into it."

165

"The Bleckflotos Secret Weapons Works?" Nick asked. "Shit! You mean they really *were* making secret weapons?"

A huge, circular shadow appeared over the point, with a tiny red jewel burning brightly at its center. Then the clouds swirled away as the *Glaurung* moved inexorably toward its destiny. The monstrously armored underside appeared, supported by a retrofitted ring of six mighty legs.

Ildenhagen cut in the distractor.

There was no flash, no sound, but the *Glaurung* began to fall. From a height of 190 meters, in Malusia's gravity of 9.92 meters/second/second, it fell for 6.22 seconds. To those watching, it seemed to fall forever, more than a million tons coming to ground on a rocky plain with a terminal velocity of 61.7 meters per second, or 222.1 kilometers per hour.

The legs, stressed far beyond their design limit, buckled, kicking up great chunks of granite, and the *Glaurung* touched down, not gently. Its huge bulk quivered, and deformed, and lay still.

"We *got* the son of a bitch!" Karff yelled exultantly.

A blue-white bolt of lightning, absolutely straight, almost vertical, flashed between the wreck of the *Glaurung* and the transporter. The thunderclap was a few milliseconds behind. The transporter shook and started to bank steeply.

Karff grabbed the phone. "Hey, Ildenhagen," he barked, "let's get *out* of here!"

"She's working on it," Pamela Gray replied, "but it isn't that simple."

"What do you *mean*?" A second vertical lightning bolt flashed, backlighting the wrecked battlecruiser to show the black cracks in the gleaming metal.

The transporter lurched again. The transporter seemed to be circling around the *Glaurung*. "There are three Rebel transporters topside," Pamela said at last. They *know* we're here. They have a fix on our FAD."

"Then why haven't they hit us?"

"Because the *Glaurung*'s FADs are—what Stavo said was 'decomposing.' They don't see us sharp, but with a kind of halo effect because of all the background noise."

"Then can't we shoot back at them?"

"Not without taking the FAD-200 out of the distractor mode," Pamela said. "That's six hours' work right there."

"Well, goddamnit, dump the FAD-200 and get out!" Karff yelled.

"I talked that over with Ildenhagen earlier," she said. "You know, the cloud cover we're under is only a few tens of meters thick."

"So what?!"

"So if we dump eighty-seven hundred kilograms of ballast, we're going to pop up like a clay pigeon and they'll pick us off by eye."

"Why didn't you bring this to my attention?" Karff asked.

"Getting the *Glaurung* was the important thing," Pamela said. "Arcziari thought something would turn up, and Captain Detana said we'd just have to play it by ear. To make a getaway, sir."

"Right." Karff sighed. "If I'd known, I might have worried about it. Carry on, Gray." A vertical lightning bolt exploded half a meter outside the window, cracking it.

"What was *that*?" Nick asked, looking up from the floor.

"A bolt of lightning. See, you can shoot things with a FAD. And when you do, you wind up with a straight line of ionized air. And if it connects two regions of different potential, why, you get an electric discharge running down the line."

"Right," Nick said. "I used to do the weather on the TV. I *know* that shit. That was maybe the tenth or twentieth thunderclap in less than a minute. Where is all the potential *coming* from?"

They went over to the broken window. They were only a few hundred meters from the wrecked battlecruiser, and through the cracks in its hull, they could see blue lights flickering.

Karff picked up the phone.

"Ahoy, the Bridge," he said. "is there any chance that that thing down there might explode?"

"He wants odds," Pamela called to someone.

"Tell him one to ten," Stavo said in the distance. "That's one to ten megatons in the next one to ten minutes."

"The son of a bitch is going to blow?" Karff asked.

"Yes, sir," Pamela said. "You heard Stavo?"

"I heard him. Are you sure we don't want to move away from it a little?"

"We have it under active consideration."

"Carry on, ma'am." The room was suddenly deathly quiet.

"...stinking bankers!" said Judith on the TV. "The blood-sucking parasites! They have held dominion over you *forever*, and now they have the insolence, the effrontery, the terminal *gall* to ask you to vote for them!!"

"*Well*," Karff said. "Nick, can you patch me through for the rally?"

Nick checked his watch. "You aren't supposed to be on for another forty minutes," he said.

"That's *her* problem. Put me through."

"*Shit*! The camera's broken! I can put you through, but it will have to be voice contact only."

"That will do, Nick. Now hurry it up!"

The crowd was chanting "Ju-dith! Ju-dith! Ju-dith!" when Nick put him through, finally.

"Good evening," he said. "This is Colonel Sir Thibalt Karff. How are you doing, Judith?"

"You can *hear* how I'm doing. *You* aren't supposed to be on for another half hour. What's up?"

"What's *down*, you mean! We brought down the *Glaurung*, Judith! The distractor program you sent over from the Bleck-flotos group did the trick!" There was a blast of thunder.

"What was that?" she asked.

"Snipers," Karff replied. "One of the reasons I called early, I might not make it another thirty minutes. Or another ten."

"Thibalt?" She hesitated. "I don't know what to say—"

"Hey, do you know the words to the 'Degradero'?"

"The Imperial Anthem? I know them."

"Good. I'll sing it one line at a time. Will you translate it, please?" He sang the first line in a passable baritone.

"'Do you hear the drum, my comrades?'" Judith said.

The *Glaurung* had started to quiver. On the Bridge of the transporter, Ildenhagen turned around to Sergeant Stavo.

"How long?" she asked.

"Less than a minute," Stavo said. "*Positively* less than two."

"The Rebel transporters are pretty high up," Detana said. "They might have trouble spotting us."

"Right," Ildenhagen said. "Here goes nothing!" She leaned over the console and hit the release switch.

The tapes holding the FAD-200 in place were cut by tiny explosive charges, as were the control cables. Stavo's instrument panel flashed red as every indicator went dead. The FAD-200, now 8,700 kilograms of ballast, slid off the cargo bay floor, through the open doors, and into the unquiet peat bog below. Pamela Gray gave the rotors full power, and the transporter shot through the thin protective layer of clouds into the night sky.

As Judith translated the next to the last line of the final stanza, a fireball brighter than a thousand suns shocked the still swampwaters, and scattered mangroves like jackstraws.

The transporter went off the air, leaving only silence crackling with static. There was a brief pause in the stadium as the eastern sky glowed green and yellow.

Then Judith sang the last line of the "Degradero" in Imperiales and spoke it in Mamnu.

"'Do not mourn that we have fallen,'" she said. "'Freedom soon will come!'"

Her voice choked on 'soon,' and 'will come' was still a whisper.

After what seemed like an eternity the blast from the *Glaurung* rolled across Malusiopolis, its thunderous fury now too diffuse to do more than rattle the windows.

The next day Judith won by a landslide.

About the Author

Born in Bangor, Maine, on August 10, 1931, Alexis A. Gilliland is a chemist by training (BS Purdue, MS Geo. Washington) and a retired bureaucrat by inertia. Formerly with the Presidential Honor Guard, the National Bureau of Standards, and the General Services Administration, he is married to Dolly, a lovely lady, and lives in Arlington, Virginia, with their son, Charles.

To date, he has been nominated for the fan artist Hugo six times, winning once, and has published a book of cartoons, *The Iron Law of Bureaucracy*. His first published fiction was *The Revolution from Rosinante* and *Long Shot for Rosinante* from Del Rey in 1981, for which he won the John W. Campbell Award for best new writer (easing him through his midlife crisis), and *The Pirates of Rosinante* in 1982.

He started reading science fiction in 1944 and entered fandom twenty years later when it became too hard to win in chess tournaments. In chess circles he was known for his wit and charm; in fandom he was known for his sharp chess playing.

His current hobby is brewing beer in his basement, the closest he has been to bench chemistry for many years.